HULME'S INVESTIGATIONS INTO THE BOGART SCRIPT

Zulfikar Ghose

PEACH PUBLISHING

By the Same Author

FICTION
The Incredible Brazilian Trilogy:
Book One: The Native
Book Two: The Beautiful Empire
Book Three: A Different World

A New History of Torments
The Contradictions
Crump's Terms
Don Bueno
Figures of Enchantment
Hulme's Investigations into the Bogart Script
The Murder of Aziz Khan
The Triple Mirror of Self
Statement against Corpses
(stories, with B. S. Johnson)
Veronica and the Góngora Passion
The Texas Inheritance
(as William Strang)

POETRY
Jets from Orange
The Loss of India
A Memory of Asia
Selected Poems
The Violent West

CRITICISM
Beckett's Company
The Fiction of Reality
The Art of Creating Fiction
Hamlet, Prufrock and Language
In the Ring of Pure Light
Shakespeare's Mortal Knowledge

Published by
Peach Publishing

To

David Edwards

and

Alessandra Lippucci

Author's Note

I have the memory of having read the following note in a text which I have not been able to re-discover:

> 'Succeeding sentences, the second explicitly or implicitly referring to the content of the first (and so on until the text is presumed to be completed), give us the impression of a continuing reality. But they are only sentences, one after the other, each itself and only itself. And grammar? All prestidigitation employs rules.'

It had been my desire to use that note as an epigraph to this work but, not having a verifiable source to quote and not wishing to appear to be imitating Stendhal's example in *Le Rouge et Le Noir* where several epigraphs are themselves fictions, I offer instead the following from two familiar texts:—

> ' . . . what the story is all about, who the protagonist may be, seems of small account beside the explosion of the particular moment . . .'

—Malcolm Lowry: *Under the Volcano*

> 'When we first begin to believe anything, what we believe is not a single proposition, it is a whole system of propositions. (Light dawns gradually over the whole.)'

—Ludwig Wittgenstein: *On Certainty*

I

A Transatlantic Prologue

Finally we arrived in the desert. The TWA flight from Heathrow to Kennedy had starred Edward G. Robinson in a color movie as some artist wearing a beret and a goatee. He looked pretty French. Sure, he lived in Paris, too, in a studio overlooking the Seine and was visited all summer by blue-dressed, over-made-up middle-aged women from such towns as Columbus, Ohio, and Pensacola, Florida, who hoped to pick up a nice little still-life of apples and chrysanthemums but invariably ran into the near-nude model and were lost for words, leaving the expression of their outraged sentiments to arched eyebrows and gasping open mouths. Not so outraged, though, since near-nudity is okay; for the middle-aged middle-brow with their package-tour processed information of the world's focal points for the Polaroid snap near-nudity is something they expect on their arrival in Honolulu, say, or in the middle of a safari in Kenya; and certainly it would be disappointing in Paris, sooner or later, not to encounter the startled model snatching at a sheet to hold on to her precious little wobblies or not being able to make the hurriedly grasped towel reach from the nipplihood of the timid breast to some decent point on the creature-comforting curvature of the barebummed embarrassment that's sending rollicking undulations in the stomachs of the used car salesmen from Little Rock, Arkansas, sucking Rolaids in the economy no-smoking section of the 747. The startled look, all blue mascara, the lost-for-words humor of middle America on its shocking travels, and here we are in dapper old Edward G. Robinson's goddamn studio in Paris, France, it's unbelievable. Maybe Edward G. wasn't wearing a beret but a toque blanche and maybe he wasn't an artist but a chef who'd authored a twenty dollar cookbook and the plot involved him in hilarious female harassments, the ladies from Columbus, Ohio,

1

etc., wanting to nibble his garlic-smelling finger-tips as if they were asparagus, and the near-nude lady was not a model but the chef's assistant who finding the 350°F temperature of the oven unbearably hot had stripped to her pink, white and blue striped undies and would have dispensed with the tricolor at her breast that seemed to flap in a kind of bosom-breeze every time she sighed, and she sighed plenty, but some sense of patriotism in the face of the fire made her keep her cool. Incredible, what goes on at forty thousand feet, even the movies are insane. There was dust on the trees in Manhattan and I said to Rosemary, What a cliché, an artist with a goddamn goatee at a time when Wall Street lawyers wear false sideburns in the evenings, and Rosemary looking out of the cab at the East River remarked, But he had a goatee in 'The Cincinnati Kid' and one hell of a poker face. I didn't even nod my head since I was looking at some black kids playing behind a wire fence and was thinking that it was the other time when I crossed the Atlantic alone that a tall youth had sat next to me, taking the aisle seat, and had said that he came from Columbus, Ohio, although he had been born in Pensacola, Florida, and his father had been a used car salesman in Little Rock, Arkansas, before the family moved to Columbus, and I thought to myself that it was worth remembering that history of now done darkness, of the air at twenty-nine thousand feet made dense by other crossings at other altitudes, for that explained what I'd mistakenly thought earlier. One thing was certain, there were a lot of facts in my head and I had a beatific sense of conviction that I knew the precise place of each fact in the phenomenological cubicles which must make such a charming doll's house in my brain. There was a sun somewhere over Manhattan, out to the west, making the buildings along the avenue throw diagonal shadows as if they were dark buttresses. The cab kept hitting the darkness, and looking at an overpass I saw cabs floating away on a yellow stream, their side-windows catching the sun, carrying the broken fragments of the sun into the beyond of their destinations. *We live in an old chaos of the sun*, I heard the poet's voice from the corners of a room where black-faced rectangular speakers stood behind potted plants, mechanical oracles, amplifying the distant memory of the race.

Of course, it was much later that we reached the desert, and for the present we did not even have the desert on our minds since we'd just been across the Atlantic. Now there was Rosemary's apartment on the seventh floor of a brick building on East 17th.

—What about that inspector? Rosemary asked, turning away from the East River to observe me framed in the cab window with, as I saw her see me, the blur of the black kids behind the wire fence while I thought that it had been a mistake leasing a car in Europe, we'd spent so many hours just sitting in the traffic. Rosemary's question drew my glance to her and for a moment I saw a tugboat on the river, hauling heaped-up trash.

—Certainly a strange case, I said, looking past Rosemary's shoulder through the rear window as if it were important to fix my glance on the tugboat and wondering why I had been sitting on the edge of the seat. I leaned back in a slouching posture, letting my head rest on the plastic upholstery.

The scream, I had said, holding the razor in my hand, is not only 'The Cry' in Edvard Munch's picture, it is also there as a motif in modern consciousness, appearing in literature and music. The plague victims in Camus's novel scream, there is a terrifying symphony of screaming voices when the boy in the ward is dying and all the other victims take up his cry, there is more than one scream in 'Guernica,' and every rock album is filled with screams as if the musicians found themselves trapped in a deadly African jungle. And you and I have seen naked Southeast Asian children on the evening newscast, running, their bodies burning with napalm, screaming. And there's the silence of the desert, too, where the emptiness between the sand and the highflying buzzards rings in your ears, sharper than pain. The scream has become such a cliché that art has turned toward silence, creating flat monochromatic dead-colored paintings, a theater of expressive pauses, a poetry that will not raise its voice—the whole din of fracturing thought scarcely makes a noise. And some who screamed the loudest took to drugs, let heroin run in their veins, stilled the rage in the throat. A deadness in the end, a glazed stare at the void, a despair that will not even communicate itself, the sweat dried up on the cold brow. We court nothingness, the capacity gone to lust after the sensual,

3

exhausted by the scream, brought to the desert in a premature conclusion of our explorations. A bubble of blood on one's chin in the morning mirror puts a period to rhetorical mumbling while the voice involuntarily curses in a whispered aside—Fuck it.

In sapphire arenas of the hills . . . ah, that vision again, that outward projection, the imagination daring to believe in its own stubborn formulations, those dazzling landscapes, dreams of apple orchards in late summer.

—I wonder what he was after, Rosemary said in a voice so without tone and looking straight ahead of her she could have been telling the cab-driver to turn right at the next corner, which was in fact what he did. She looked at me when I said nothing and then turned her eyes away.

—That inspector, she added.

Beware, I had told myself while speaking (but that was across the Atlantic in another world while here only the yellow cabs), of anti-rhetorical rhetoric. We pursue words like cops some anonymous caller's hoax. That was when I saw him, the stockily-built middle-aged man who was taking notes. A journalist probably, I thought while I said—I was away for a fortnight recently and on returning found a dead bird in my study, it had obviously come in through the chimney and found itself trapped. There was birdshit on my desk, on some books that lay on a couch, on some cushions, on an old wooden rocking chair, on the speakers behind the potted plants, on the floor. It must have hurled itself at the window-panes, flown around desperately in the closed room. I do not know if birds scream, but seeing it lying dead, seeing its shit all around the room, I heard the wild beating of its wings, seeing the white spots and streaks, the abstraction of form that configured despair. But as I spoke, I thought the stockily-built man with the veined purple-splotched pink cheeks could not be a journalist, for who would want to report an argument of despair? Afterwards, on another occasion, I almost met him.

I was in a gallery in Cork Street and a young eager-voiced dealer named Cecil Paltry-Smith, his accent so Oxbridgey it could only have been the affectation of one who'd graduated from Hull or Lancaster, was showing me a portfolio of prints that I'd especially requested to see. There were mirrors in the corners of the gallery so that the two assistants could keep the three rooms under surveillance and while Mr Tawdry-Smith turned the prints over, keeping up a laudatory commentary upon the artist's work, I saw the figure in the mirror that I thought I recognized. Mr Powdery-Smith saw him, too, and said, Ah, Inspector Hulme! I trust, he added, laughing, the Obscenity Act is not the occasion of your visit.

The drooping moustache upon Inspector Hulme's upper lip straightened very slightly to indicate something of a smile, but he did not say anything as he walked toward Mr Poultry-Smith, his eyes taking a sweeping glance at the pictures on the wall. While he walked, I thanked Mr Coterie-Smith for the trouble he'd taken to show me the portfolio and saying that I'd like some time for reflection before deciding what I wished to purchase, for new art, I added, needed as he well knew more than a cursory, and he interrupted me with Yes, yes, of course, concluding which amiable exchange, I walked away through a narrow passage where a sequence of framed lithographs covered the walls, grey and black the dominant color. I was walking too quickly to see any detail in the prints, one picture fusing into the next one with each step I took, grey-black merging into grey-black, so that the passage had the effect of a tunnel on my mind until I emerged into the grey-white light of the street.

I walked from Cork Street to Green Park tube station, cutting across Bond Street and pausing at a pub on a corner either on Dover Street or Albemarle Street—a Dukish pub with some regimental arms militarily gasconading around the bar and the young fledgeling, Mr Jeremy Titt, who stood at the counter with his ridiculous handle-bar moustache behind the plastic casks for the draught beer, and who on my asking if he had any pickled gherkins or potato crisps said We don't have that soat o' thing hyah (so that I gave him a stare as if to say, Look, Mr Jeremy Pricke, don't give me that bloody la-di-dah, for I know your kind of class which takes on the murky airs of the upperclassy nimbypamby-ness). I bought the evening paper outside Henly's car showroom, seeing the headline about the kidnap-rape-murder at the same time as I descended into the underground.

I began reading the story going down the escalator, switching my attention from the kidnap details to look at the laced-up bosoms on the corset and vodka ads along the escalator. Miss Vee Hayter-Overy, a model—and I saw just then the framed ad beside the escalator of bikini-bosomed Miss Nubilette Boobs in the Mediterranean at Tunis barely concealing her Christian boobiloos in a world of tense Arab tumidity—had been kidnapped from the studio in Frith Street just when she was posing in front of a plastic palm-tree and the painted blue waters of the sea on the coast of North Africa. It was the usual story which held me with the usual absorption. And it was not until I'd secured a seat in the Piccadilly Line going to Piccadilly Circus and beyond that I reached the end of the story and was struck by the concluding statement: Inspector Hulme is leading the investigation into the extraordinary circumstances surrounding the case which involve such puzzlingly disparate factors as a desert tribe, jet-setting movie stars, and the world of art. When I read that, the train stopped at Piccadilly Circus, and I realized that although I'd been aware when catching the train that it was going to Piccadilly Circus, that was not the direction I'd wanted to take since I needed to go to South Kensington, and I wondered why I had not been able to check myself when I knew the wrongness of my direction.

—It's always the same, Rosemary said, but another voice, one so wearied by autochthonous wisdom that his speech is slurred, echoed gloomily *as if the earth under our feet were an excrement of some sky*, so that I missed what else Rosemary said and she added after a pause, Don't you agree?

But there was the surprise of the cardboard cutout Manhattan skyline in the August sunlight and the invisible swirlings of dust and soot, that particular mirage of the city which provoked an immediate surrender of reason. *Some dim inheritance of sand . . . old chimera of the grave* called voices from some ocean-depth or some desert: *here, now, always*—the fouled-up flesh rising to compose itself for a comprehensive journey. Who could stop them, the noble insistences of the human voice, the phrases of incomprehensible beauty? *But heard, half-heard, in the stillness* even in these Manhattan noises, the traffic pursuing its busy directions, the police sirens.

Rain, soft rain in London. Buying tickets one morning at a theater, I saw a sign beside a door next to the box-office: QUIET PLEASE REHEARSAL IN PROGRESS. There was only a heavy velvet curtain across the door and no one to stop me. I took a seat in the back row. On the brightly-lit stage, a man and a woman sat on bar-stools some ten feet from each other, facing the auditorium, the stage otherwise empty. A number of people sat in the front stalls, scattered here and there in slouching positions or with arms over the adjacent seat-backs or legs over the seat at the front. One sat upright on the seat far to the right some five or six rows from the front. The couple on the stage remained silent, staring into the distance with emotionless eyes. He thin, emaciated, chalk-white face and boney hands; she fleshed enough for dimples at the cheeks, her cuddlicoops roundly filling a sweater of grey lambswool. NOW shouted a voice from above, someone in the dress-circle, and she in a voice as clear as the Colorado sky: I remember. A pause. And she again:

A barn in Somerset. Or a sand-dune in Cornwall.
(Pause).
Was it the old wooden door that creaked?
Or was it the wind caught in a crack in the sky over
Cornwall? I remember distinctly a vagueness.
(Pause).
I remember.
(Long pause).

And he in his skull-and-bones voice, a hollow rasping:

The clouds were manes I held on to as
I rode the wind, mounted on the
oxblood saddle of the sun. My arms
were silver as trout in crystal streams.

STOP THERE! shouted the voice upstairs. Two or three of the heads in the front stalls looked back and up, and the voice said, I say, Keith, can't you change that fucking line? I mean what have

7

fucking trout got to do with the image of the rider in the bleeding sky? I'm sorry, George, a man in the stalls, presumably Keith, replied, but it's the shock of the contradiction that I'm after. But TROUT for chrissake, shouted the man upstairs, I mean trout are so fucking tiny. But THAT is the point, argued Keith, the insignificant weak little creature is given power. Oh, JESUS! shouted George, don't you see it's too fucking EARLY in the play for that kind of thing? I don't think so, said Keith, I'm not Terence bloody Rattigan for God's sake!

While this argument proceeded, the man sitting on the far right some five or six rows from the front rose and walked up the aisle and out of the door near to where I was sitting. He was wearing a raincoat and had put on a felt hat. Even in silhouette I would have recognized him as Inspector Hulme but I saw his face, the drooping moustache and that look in his eye that indicated he was puzzling over something, carrying on some inner dialogue, and could have no doubt about his identity. I left soon after, almost following him out, but by the time I emerged from the theater he was nowhere to be seen.

Rosemary had seen him in Queen Elizabeth Hall when she'd gone to listen to something by Schoenberg. Not having an ear for music, I'd stayed in the hotel watching TV, some Western movie about a wagon-train running into Indians before finally making it to Santa Fe. Of course, Rosemary had no way of knowing that I'd seen Hulme before or whether the Hulme she saw was the Hulme I'd seen or even whether the man she saw was indeed Hulme. In fact, she said nothing about Hulme when she returned from the concert. She didn't want to talk, she was still hearing the music. I switched off the TV and went out for a walk, thinking about Danny Pickett who coveted Joe Ferguson's girl Jeanie of high nubility and told Jeanie that Joe was an outlaw from St Louis, which was a lie, while Danny himself slipped out at night to tell the Indians how they could kill Joe Ferguson and wipe out the wagon-train with him, but of course everyone got to Santa Fe except Danny who was killed by an arrow aimed at Joe, so it was okay even though Joe had a wound in his left shoulder, that's what I did, walked out for a couple of hours leaving Rosemary to her musical echoes. But the next day when we were going out together I picked up the morning paper in the hotel lobby and when I opened the paper in the cab there was Hulme's picture on the second page, for apparently he was still investigating some famous crime, and a quotation in which he said that the clues so far had been rather vague. Rosemary happened to see the picture while I read the article and said, Why, that man was at the concert last night! I noticed him because he had a manner about him that bothered me. I don't know what it was. Just a concentrated look in his eyes, like someone who's drunk too much and is consciously trying to look sober. He was standing by the door during the interval. I wouldn't have seen him but I wanted to go to the rest room and for a moment our eyes met as I went past him, and I said to myself, Goodness he looks the picture of G. K. Chesterton.

I described how I'd seen him at railway stations, airport terminals, phone booths, car rental offices, art galleries, street-corners, museums, theaters, universities, cathedrals, ancient ruins, movies, night clubs, restaurants, ocean liners, jumbo jets, local buses, hotel lobbies, mirrors, dreams. I expect he'll be on the plane to New York, too, I added.

Actually, I looked when we boarded the plane at Heathrow. We'd been talking about him while we sat out the two-hour delay, drinking Scotch in the departures lounge. But the Boeing was full of big-waisted middle Americans on their way back from Edward G. Robinson's studio in Paris. They looked pretty worn out after their trials with foreign currencies. There were the stewardesses, nothing pneumatic about their tightly bra'd thimblifoos, fluttering about in their eau de cologne world as if there could be no questions.

There was a pile of mail for Rosemary at her apartment. She'd arranged for her friend Pru Essenfoot from the apartment below hers to pick it up from her box to save herself the bother of having to go to the post-office to have it stopped. A lot of it was junk mail—special offers on magazines, book clubs, group travel invitations to see the Monte Carlo Grand Prix or a beer festival in Munich or the Taj Mahal in moonlight or the film festival in Cannes or the Turdification festival of Constantipation, etc.,

etc. One of the bits of junk mail was a printed invitation from her alma mater on Long Island, to whose mailing list of exes she perversely belonged, announcing a lecture on investigative procedures by Inspector Hulme.

II

The Lady on the Staircase

Shimmered hazily in the sun early summer in the Southwest, the wistful chickenhawks riding high the blue air. Powdery and white, chalky dust compacted, the limestone outcrops. For a moment, on a white rock beside a cedar tree, a green lizard with a translucent tail worked his throat into distended pink aggression and then slipped into the tree's shadow.

Driven by ethereal rumors, intoxications carried by aircurrents on summer-scented routes, the crazed hummingbird darts from the high mimosa to the mauve horsemint rising from the underbrush. Beyond the cedar and mimosa hill the fields of gaillardia, scarlet and yellow, whose pointillist intensity overwhelmingly routs the splashes of mauve and purple horsemint, verbena and spiderwort. And this in the pebbly, chalky soil in the tensed thighs of the bright-eyed land. And this, too, the last riot, for here the seasonal promiscuities of rain are violent in their transient and chance violations, leaving the land first puddled, then parched, and then this eruption of red and yellow and mauve and purple.

There is no clamor for the sun here which is both a universal comforter and a whimsical killer. Beyond, the desert. Past the gaillardia where the flowers, too, whiten, the green milkweed and milfoil and Queen Anne's-lace turning ghostly, these blendings into the earth's moods, past the milfoil's proud composure in a straitened world, the solider rocks are already implacably positioned. Here and there a burnt cedar-trunk, but the rocks are already the executioners, guardians of the desert. Beyond, the dust: narcissistic and whirling in extravagant terpsichorean expressions of self-love, rousing itself in spiralling frenzies, taking giddy possessions of space, tearing itself to its bare atoms in an endless jactation of its own endurance. Dust, dust . . . *straddling spontaneities that form their independent orbits* ... the perpetuity of self-motion, the final barrenness.

I sat on a rock under the mimosa tree, and saw the hummingbird suddenly appear from the air and balance itself in front of the mimosa blossom for a moment before turning its little head and propelling itself away, like an Ariel plunging through space to encircle the earth during the twinkling of an eye, when I saw it again twenty yards away down the hill examining the red poppy-like blossoms of a prickly-pear cactus.

—Did you see that? I asked my horse Gary whom I'd tied to a cedar tree while we rested from the afternoon heat. Gary stood dazed, his brown coat streaked black with sweat. I'd purchased him in Nashville when of the six horses in the stable he'd been the only one to turn his head and look at me when I'd said, Well, who'd like to ride out West with me? I'd wanted a horse with a sense of ambition.

And when we rode out across the river valleys of west Tennessee, through the morning fog and the lovely early spring afternoons of glinting Irish-green hills, I'd said to him, Okay, my boy, I'll call you Gary after the guy in the old West in the mining town in Nevada who didn't give a spittin' damn for the trigger-happy Saturday night drunks but took 'em on with his bare fists to make it a safe place for the long-skirted and bonnetted ladies, how about that, eh? It was a kind of no-protest election, and I said, Well, since you don't say nuthin', I guess it's okay with you, but let me tell you, fella, anytime you feel like a change I'll understand, just give me the old neigh.

We rode across the plains of Arkansas and through the pine forest of northeast Texas. It was a green land mostly until we reached here where coming over the hill and stopping for a rest, there was the field of wild flowers below, a million dots of red and yellow and mauve and purple. I just sat there taking the colors in as if I were fixing to do a painting like a painting I'd seen of cowboys chasing steers in the long grass in the mayor's office in Little Rock, a cactus in the corner of the picture and a round yellow sun at the top.

The hummingbird shot away from the red poppy blossoms of

the prickly-pear cactus and soon could not be distinguished from the specks of dust in the air. I mounted Gary and took a path down into the valley. We headed west again, across a field of wild flowers, out to the plain where the trees were no higher than my line of vision. Soon there were more rocks than trees. And there on the horizon was the frame-house, just beside the sunset.

It was dark by the time I reached the house. I guess she had seen me coming from a distance, for she had left a lit lamp in the front porch. The wick was too high, and the chimney was smoking. I turned it low before I entered, hearing her voice call, Is that you, Walt?

—Sure, maw, it's me, I said, going in. She sat by a fire of live-oaks, and I added, Where you get the wood from, Poker? Looks like good live-oak to me.

She rose when I called her by her nick-name, and said, Well, if it ain't wandering Walt come back!

—Sure, it's me, you saw me coming, didn't you?

—Yeah, it's live-oak, she said. Willie Burnett brought it me in his wagon. There's beer in the ice-box, she added, sitting down by the fire again, I put a quart in the freezer section when I saw you was comin'. You'll find it by the packet of frozen peas. It should be pretty iced by now. And there's some dinner in the oven. Turn the knob to broil and switch it to four hundred and it'll be done in twenty minutes. It's sealed, she emphasised, in aluminum foil. Willie Burnett was on his way to Phoenix, Arizona, if you want to know. Some insurance business there, he said.

I fetched the beer and sat down at the large kitchen table in the middle of the room, a lamp of polished copper hanging from the ceiling over the table, its flame turned down so that it burned real soft.

Poker Hortense looked at me from her rocking chair by the fire. She was tall and erect when she stood up but appeared to be a fragile old woman in the chair, her face furrowed and webbed with wrinkles. Naturally, I never knew her early youth when she had dark straight hair and was called Happy Hortense, being the kind of girl who never thinks anyone could want to take advantage of her. Men came and loved her, and she let them

13

come, smiling. Out in the cotton fields or deep within the timber forests or at sunset on the prairie with a million buffaloes on the horizon or beside the great lakes or up above the snowline on the Rockies, wherever she was, she didn't mind the men who took her. That's how she got the name Poker. Anyone could poke her, it was okay with her. One time she dyed her hair blond and joined a line of chorus girls kicking their legs at the men in the saloon in Santa Fe, joining the men at the card-table after the act, which was another reason why she was called Poker Hortense, for she played poker like no woman ever did in the West. There was the famous night in Denver when she won fifty-five grand playing the legendary Arizona Bobbie who'd never lost a nickel in his life, and it was said that in the last game all she had was a pair of twos but holding the mean hand to her bosom she stared the sweat outta Bobbie's ass. I learned these things about her many years ago when she was already old. I'd always known her old.

—Did you set the timer on that range? she asked.

—No, ma'am, I didn't, I said, leaning back in my chair and emptying the glass of beer down my throat.

—How'll you know it's twenty minutes?

—I got my eye on the clock, don't you worry.

—Pay no heed to that clock, it's fast.

—That's okay, I said. I don't want to know the time, only that twenty minutes have passed.

—It gains two hours a day, she said, that's five minutes in every hour or two and a half minutes in every thirty minutes. You won't be able to tell twenty minutes by looking at twenty minutes go by on that clock.

—That's okay, too, I said. I have a watch in my pocket. I can check with that. Say, I said, looking at my watch, your clock isn't two hours fast, it's nearly five hours slow. I make it twenty after eight and your clock shows just gone three.

—I told you not to go by it, she said. It's crazy. It's been going at that hopped-up speed since the time they hit gold in California. Those were the days, Walt, everything went at a hell of a speed, it was difficult to keep track of time. Now I never even look at it, except to wind it.

I unsealed the aluminum foil and found two pork chops surrounded by lima beans, four sections of tomato and a two-inch piece of celery, all covered with apple sauce.

—Here, Poker said when I began to eat, you might like to try a glass of this Gallo Hearty Burgundy I picked up for 99 cents at Safeway. You couldn't get vin ordinaire at this price even if you'd driven to Rouen in your rented Citroën.

—You're right, I said, pouring myself a glass of the Gallo, I was in Carpentras last summer and I'd just bought some groceries and when I was paying for them to the man who looked like he'd once owned a brothel in New Orleans my eye caught some vin ordinaire on the counter and I said to him, Say, how much is a bottle of that ordinaire? And he said, A dollar twenty. What do you mean a dollar twenty, I said, I'm paying in francs as you can see. I just want you to know, he said, what it's worth in your money to save you the bother of converting from francs to find out how it compares with Gallo.

—What does a guy look like who's owned a brothel in New Orleans? Poker asked.

—Long sideburns, clipped moustache, black hair glossy with vaseline, and a husky voice.

—O, said Poker, you must be referring to the nineteenth century.

—Maybe, I said, chewing the pork chop which was pretty tender. That's the way Clark Gable played it.

—What was he doing in Carpentras? Poker asked.

—I asked him that, I said. He said he'd come south from Lyons, he didn't like the industrialisation there, the factories got on his nerves, there was too much mugging, and school kids were taking dope.

—He should have stayed in New Orleans, Poker said. Go ahead, have another glass if you like it that much, consider it your own vineyard.

—Poker, I said, I remember how by the Colorado river once we had a picnic of smoked eel and André's Cold Duck. You were mighty pretty then with your red hair in curls around your ears, little ringlets on the corners of your forehead, and your blue eyes deeper than the sky over the Rockies.

15

—I'd flown over from Denver to meet you, she said. Remember, you met me at the airport in your white Lincoln, you were wearing a white linen suit and a white panama hat you'd bought on a trip to Florida. You drove at a hundred and twenty miles an hour on the highway across the flat nearly desert country and you had the car stereo playing Pat Boone and Rosemary Clooney.

—Jesus, that was a long time ago, I said.

—It was yesterday, Walt, yesterday.

—And you wore a long dress with little pink flowers on it, and a pink waistband, and you were barefooted, I saw you come off that plane in your naked feet, that was pretty sensational, Poker. I don't know if I'd play the same music again, though, I added after a pause.

—Boy, did you have passion in those days! Poker said. You could do things in those days.

—Sure, I was real eager, I said.

—Hortense, you said, taking my breasts gently in your hands.

—Hortense, I said.

—Sure, you were eager, you had passionate eyes, you could see I was worth conquering.

—Poker Hortense, I said, I'd come to you now, take your long straight black hair in my hands and put my mouth to your white neck and love you with my original ardor, but I ate too much, didn't need that second chop, you shouldn't have given me so much, and the Gallo's making me drowsy.

—Yeah, I can see that, she said, your eyes have a heavy look. Your bed's made up, if you want to go to sleep.

—I think I'll do that, I said, finishing the last of the wine. Maybe I'll come to you in the morning. I'll brew some coffee and bring you a cup and come and lie next to you.

—I put brand-new sheets on your bed, she said. They're green, blue and brown stripes. Pillowcase, towels and bathroom tissue to match.

—Am I tired! I said, rising.

—There's a creek at the back of the house, Poker said, which you can bathe in, if you like. In the morning. The water comes down from the Rockies. It's real cool.

16

—I swam in the Mississippi by Memphis the other day, I said.

—Just south of Memphis where there are willows, Poker said. Sure, you swam in the Mississippi. I jumped off the boat first, remember?

—You had nothing on, I said, and there was a steamer coming up the river and you dived deep down into the water. I dived after you, pursuing the phosphorescent glow of your body upon the current that took you down to the riverbed, there among the reeds and the little fish and the broken bottles.

—That creek's okay, she said. It's clear, clean water, real cool, too. The buffalo drink from it downstream and there's a brewery that uses it to make beer.

I went to my room, took a quick shower, switched on the TV at the foot of the bed and went to sleep. Bruce Janssen, having driven all night from Sacramento, was having breakfast with Moyra Delaney in a cabin in the Rockies. He had removed his coat and sat in his vest and shirt, the sleeves buttoned at the wrists, two revolvers by his arm-pits. He had stood by the window while Moyra was bringing the boiling pot of coffee to the table and had looked down at the stream that tumbled downhill not far from the cabin, the high sierra rising beyond the valley. There were birds singing and Bruce, walking to the table just when Moyra had set the plates with ham and eggs on the table, said, I guess it could be a good life out here, eh, honey? Moyra's moist lipsticked mouth quivered a moment before she said, O Bruce!, turning her nearly tearful eyes away from the coffee-pot. Eh, baby, Bruce said, having begun to cut his ham and now putting his knife down, demanded: I said it will be all right, didn't I? Yes, Bruce, Moyra said, her eyes glistening and her voice almost a whisper, as she poured out the coffee. Look sweetheart, Bruce said, standing up, abandoning the breakfast, I've made it, haven't I? All the way west, haven't I? He began to pace up and down, speaking rapidly: All we need is a piece of land, some cattle maybe, a land where the pasture's good, where the rain comes by special delivery from heaven and turns the grass green like it is in paradise, in Montana maybe or Wyoming, we've got everything now, sweetheart, all we need is a piece of land. Even as he was speaking, Moyra said, coldly,

17

despairingly, We're still on the run, Bruce, don't you see that, we're still on the run! Nobody's going to get me I tell ya, Bruce shouted back, still walking up and down, but with greater agitation in his steps and a scowl upon his face. I outrode them out of Dodge City, remember, I made monkeys of them out of Sacramento last night, I bet they're still headin' for L.A. Moyra rose from the table and walked toward him, saying, O Bruce! At that moment Bruce had come to a stop by the window and was turning around. He stood still for a moment looking at Moyra, saying O baby!, with his back to the window. Just then a burst of machine-gun fire sent seven bullets through his back and head and one bullet through Moyra's left shoulder who, falling, said O Bruce! Outside the sky had suddenly become clouded and a blizzard had commenced. Three cars stood by the cabin, their motors running, their doors open, bleeps and incomprehensible radio messages filling the air.

The land spread out in great sweeping arcs. Rocks stood high above the deep snowdrifts but past the sheer falls, deep below the cliffsides of shining ice, and beyond the pine-forested slopes that outdistanced a week's horizons, dropping one past the other, there were the great sweeping arcs of the land tall in summer with grass, the black shining backs of the buffalo scarcely clearing the top of the grass. The land levelled out till its rushing streams became quiet-flowing rivers from whose banks meadows rolled away toward blue distances, the dark rivers over which willows arched trailing their long mourning branches that touching the water scarcely broke its opacity. The meadows rolled away toward the bluish haze where the sequined and beaded air shimmered in the gathering waves of heat and projected fluid and convoluted chimeras across the farther horizon. The heat dragged the vegetation to its knees, the grass completely flattened and withered, little bushes with daringly red berries, but more and more of dry chalk-colored land where skulls and bones might be discovered scattered among the flints and pebbles and sand of the soil asserted itself, the strict austerity of one vast, subjugating final tone. The shimmering horizon was the edge of the lake, its shores of white dust like sandy beaches, its waters blue and ocean-deep, and from its dusty beach having oceanic proportions. South and east of the lake a few barren hills rose feebly, desperately and then the land flattened out absolutely and if anything rose from its uncompromising flatness it was only dust.

Kicking up a cloud of dust, they came to town, Archie Mozzer, Scott Bixler and the boys, spurring their horses the last quarter mile, coming to town for their whiskey 'n' women night, stroke 'em and poke 'em hilarity in the saloon, come from the silver mines among the mountains where not a blade of grass grew to give a man any kind of comfort. Come to lean back in chairs, hats tilted, cowboy boots against the edge of the table, whiskey in hand, lips pouting, come to throw the old bloodshot lustful eye at Nancy and Marilu and Jo Anne dancing there with red feathers in their hair, kicking their legs and sticking up their asses and giving the bountiful boobledoms the good old wobble. Come to get the desert out of their throats, the boys, to let fantastic rivers flow there, driven toward a varied topography. And now the horses are hitched outside the saloon, the doors swing open and Archie Mozzer swaggers in, tall in brown leather, a firm square jaw inclining to the left and to the right to let the narrow eyes check out the scene, what the action is, boys, and Scott Bixler follows on his heels, six feet tall in a brown leather jacket speckled with dust, narrowed blue eyes giving the saloon the once over, and the boys too, and head for the bar where Joe, the barkeeper, is wiping a glass, his black hair parted at the middle and his moustache waxed to needle points so that everyone calls Joe by his nick-name, Needles.

—Hi, Archie, Scott, says Needles, hi Gary, Greg, fellas, how are ya'll?

—Howdy, Needles!

—Come for a good time, fellas? asks Needles, putting the glasses and a bottle of whiskey on the counter. How's the silver? Coming out of your ears, hey, ha, ha. I wish it came outta mine!

—Jesus, we even shit silver, says Gary.

—Yeah, Needles, says Scott, you sure are welcome to clean up after us.

The boys explode with laughter. The first glasses are swallowed with a quick gesture of the hand throwing the drink back down the tilted head. Laughter explodes afresh after another variation of the same essential joke. The good time has begun, the funtime that must lead to Martha's milkwhite mummidums or Nancy's two little niceties.

—But let me tell you, fellas, says Needles, looking all serious, this is a clean place.

Ho, ho, the laughter.

But before the high bosomline breasts the waves of cigar-smoke in the room and a sweet soprano chorus infuses the veins of men with honey, Ladies and Gentlemen, announces Muscular Charlie, pray silence for the Shakespirrian actor come for your dereliction from London town, Mr Gerald Holmes, known to the court of King GeorgeWilliamCharles where for the deleterious hoopla of the Lords and Ladies the said Gerald Holmes Esquire has given unforgettable performances in tragedy and comedy, and before Muscular Charlie can finish his pomp and circumstance speech and let the imaginary trumpet raise a curtain the Voice is already declaring that it has come to bury Caesar not to praise him. Archie Mozzer and Scott Bixler and the boys having their own ambitious circum-caesars to bury listen for ten words and begin to repeat mockingly the words of the bardic Holmes, cutting the air with gesticulations, so that Needles says, Okay, cool it, fellas, cool it. Shi-eet, says Gary, drawing his gun, removing a cork from a bottle, throwing the cork up into the air and shooting it like it was a pigeon. A gambler behind the cigar-smoke at a table looks up from his cards, draws his gun and fires three shots, bang-bang-bang, at three glasses in a row behind Needles. Back in a room where Marilu is standing in a corset before a mirror putting on a red feather in her hair and beside her Nancy pulling at her own corset which is pressing too tightly at her left nautilus and on a chair Jo Anne putting on her stockings, the right leg stretched out, the left leg raised and bent at the knee, suddenly the girls hear the shots and Marilu drops her feather, Nancy tears away the corset at the front and Jo Anne falls off her chair and just then Martha bursts into the room saying, I told Charlie it was the wrong goddamn act!

Ah, screw this, I said, turning in bed and looking out of the window past the bougainvillea blooms toward the line of palms that stood along the road. Patulous bushes of red and pink and white oleander filled up the spaces between the palm trees, blossoms on every branch, and formed a fence for the citrus grove behind the road. The orange trees were small and ranged in rows that extended for miles, so that the land was flat and green, speckled with oranges that appeared as blobs and gradually receded until they were specks, minute dots from the point of a very fine brush. A red Italian sports car, its top down, sped along the road, cutting along the base of the palms and the oleanders. The blondhaired man who drove it shifted down thrice to hit second gear, little puffs of smoke being ejected from the exhaust each time he shifted, and turned into the driveway of the house, accelerated without changing gear so that the engine roared at high revs and the car shot toward the house. The man braked hard and brought the car to a stop in front of the steps outside the front door. He got out of the car and slammed the door shut and stood by the car. He gave the impression that he would have gone running up the steps and banged on the door with his fists and that he had been halted by the fact that the person he had come to see had already emerged from the house. The blondhaired man wore a white double-breasted suit with a pink shirt and a tie of a darker pink. He was tall, broad-shouldered and had a striking face with an aquiline nose and dark blue eyes that convinced anyone turning the pages of the glossy magazine that the cigarette he was smoking offered the highest gratification or that the Oldsmobile Cutlass beside which he stood in informal conversation with a young lady with flowing dark hair and a long-sleeved satin gown beside a moonlit beach was Detroit's finest achievement. The man who had come out of the house had a white beard and thick white hair.

—Jason, said the old man standing firmly in front of the door that he had closed behind him, I forbid you!

—It's my house, papa, Jason said. Remember what you used to say when I was a little boy? You'd drive back from the vineyards in the evening ...

—I know, I know, said the old man, I used to hold you on my knee as I sat out here in the porch with a glass of wine and say ...

—This is your house, you'd say, Jason said.

—No, Jason, no! the old man said, regretting his own history in an exclamation mark.

—Well, I've come back to claim my house, Jason said.

—You turned away from all this, Jason.

—At that time I didn't know who I was, Jason said. I left the house because you were my father and I had to leave you, I had to go and see the world for myself. A world without a father. Don't you understand that?

—I know why you've come back now, Jason. O Jason, don't, don't do this to your mother!

—I don't know what I'm doing to anyone. No one gave a damn what they did to me.

—It wasn't your mother's fault, Jason. I never blamed her for it. I always loved her, Jason. Don't do this to her!

A few windows away a curtain had been held back a little and a woman's face looked out: she wore a black shawl about her head, and her long face was stained with tears.

Just then a British sports car with the top down came tearing up the drive and braked to a sudden stop within an inch of the earlier parked car. A young girl, dressed for tennis, swung her bare legs out, her perfect teeth flashed as she smiled, saying, Hi, Jason, just heard you'd returned, dimples appearing at her cheeks, her pageboy hair bouncing.

—Why, it's Kathy! exclaimed Jason, looking her up and down, mainly up. You sure have grown, Kathy!

Ah, Christ! I said, feeling downright lousy, okay, okay, so Kathy is the citrus-growing neighbor's daughter who's grown into a ripe cliché with a couple of banalities bouncing in front of her, while Jason we know everything about now, so what follows is strictly mathematical, viz., the old man can no longer stand there but must admit the young couple since Kathy takes it as natural that Jason is about to go in and so she must enter, too. Alternatively, Jason says, I'd love to see you play tennis, Kathy, let's go! And off they go at two hundred miles an hour with Jason driving and Kathy saying, You sure have a firm touch, the handling's beautiful, you take a good line through the curves, and such profound ambiguities that would shock the citrus growers at their annual convention in San Diego. And it is possible that in the meantime the old man going back into the house sits sadly down by the fire and the woman with the black shawl comes up to him and places her hand on his shoulder, neither saying what the other is thinking of and each knowing that the other is thinking that Kathy who thinks she's the citrus-growing neighbor's little girl is really this old man's daughter, for when he was young, etcetera, and Jason doesn't know that therefore Kathy is his half-sister, whereas Kathy doesn't know that Jason is not this old man's son, for the woman in the black shawl was once etcetera, and that, woe, tragedy, how it all comes about, one error upon another, etshitera, and, as I was saying, O God what a civilization, these goddamn solemnities of mankind, etshitera, these miserable dramas of inconsequentiality, etshitera, these banalities packaged in the idiom of common comprehension, etshitera.

Holmes, however, was inconsolable, and wore his Richard II visage, sitting alone in a shattered saloon. Martha entered, still carrying the broom she had picked up to defend the ladies' quarters but the men had been content with splintering timber, smashing glass, the thud of fists against jaws, and the smell of blood had been as provocative as a whore's perfume worn ever so close to the nibblies.

—Some show, said Martha, you brought the goddamn house down.

—Ah, lady, could I but tell you, spoke Holmes in his Rhapsodic Voice from the early comedies, that here lies a heart worse slain than the buffalo in Montana, what compassionate fire would not burn in those wondrous jewels some men call your eyes!

—You're a fraud, Gerald, Martha said, you never were an actor, and Holmes isn't your name, is it?

—Your profile, lady, could belong to an Egyptian queen.

—Okay, sweetie, what's your game now? asked Martha. I said you're a fraud, what do you say to that? Huh?

—That did I but possess India, I should cede it to your arms.

—You can stuff the Khyber Pahse up your jolly English ahse, sweetheart, you're no actor, even I can see that, you wouldn't be tramping about the West if you were an actor.

23

—I'm an inspector of men's souls, I sit in corners of rooms, unwanted as conscience, I'm the memory that keeps returning of things not done, or things ill done, I'm the unquenchable thirst in the throat of the alcoholic, I, lady, put on elaborate masks to look behind the common masks of mankind.

—You lousy drunk! said Martha, scornfully brandishing the broom as she walked away, so that Holmes, having begun a speech, was obliged to declaim one more soliloquy: I am seeking, lady, seeking. It's hard, having seen so much and with so much still to see. And where have I come after the long journey of my rebirth, to witness what processions of the dead?

Where rivers imperceptibly slide across the swampy land; where creatures have their bellies to the slimey earth, snakes and alligators; where there are sore-lipped fissures in the earth, entrances for the bats' home; where the sun touches the surface of the rivers and sucks up foul-smelling vapors; where there's a deadly stillness and whatever moves is a killer.

Where mornings are stillborn, *some silver-fingered fountain steals the world.*

As if one lived on an island that daily, at an unpredictable hour, was hit by a tidal-wave.

—Poker, I said, sitting beside her bed, having taken her a breakfast of English muffins and Keiller's Dundee marmalade and a pot of Indian tea, there are terrible things going on in this country.

—Sure, she said, waiting for the muffin to pop out of the toaster on the bedside table, but I wish you'd brought me honey and coffee instead of marmalade and tea, who do you think I am, Queen Victoria!

—Oh, I'm sorry, Poker, I thought you'd welcome a change on a Sunday morning.

—Yeah, terrible things, she said. You had a bad night, I guess.

—So-so, I said. Not bad, really. Just a couple of nightmares.

—You're the darndest kid I ever saw, she said.

—You look great, Poker, I said. Just like Colorado in summer, a man could lie on the grass on the river-bank and think he was never happier.

—Oh, go on, Walt, come and lie with me if that's what's on your mind.

—You look just fine, I said.

—I figured, she said.

—What?

—Bullshit, she said, spreading butter on a muffin. A ranch full of bullshit, that's what I figured.

—I just like looking at you, that's all, I said. Like the centerfold in Playboy. I get a kick just looking.

—Sure, kid.

—Oh, come on, I said, I can too, if you want me to prove it.

—Spare me the drama, Walt, she said when she saw me rise and begin to take my shirt off. I don't want your goddamn proof. It's phoney.

—You're, shall we say, temperamental?

—Cut the talk, she said. This is a lousy drink. Go make me some coffee if you want to prove anything.

—Poker Hortense, you are temperamental.

—Cut it.

It wasn't that I didn't desire to go lie with her. I'd done that before on many a morning, rising early because the sun was up over the lake and the light brightened each moment in the perfect transparency of air over the still water; and whenever I awoke before her, I went and made breakfast, always something unusual, fried lamb's kidney once, a grilled chop another time, or maybe a Spanish omelette, and brought it to her on a blue plastic tray. I'd get into bed, too, and we'd eat breakfast like we were in the Plaza. Right now, though, I didn't want to get into bed and lie next to her for I knew what would happen once we'd eaten the muffins. I'd yawn and slip lower in the bed and curl up around Poker and she'd sigh with her warm breath against my neck. I'd sleep the rest of the morning, curled around her.

—You lazy good-for-nothing slob, she said.

—Ah, Poker!

—Look at you, she cried. Grown fat and empty-headed, just look at you! Bitty little eyes sunk so far back it's a wonder you can see anything at all. Round baby-face with pink rubbery cheeks, glistening hairless chin, Jesus, what a prospect for American womanhood! Narrow rounded shoulders, flabby tits and a stomach the size of a Buick's trunk, fold upon fold of fat. And down there, beyond the fat bulge of buoyant belly where you can't even see it is the sickly prickly, the eeny-meany tiny peeny with a coupla goddamn peanuts stuck under it not big enough for a golliwog's balliwogs. One hell of a prospect! Come, ladies of Oklahoma and Kansas, here is Walt the breathless performer, come, maidens of Nebraska and Indiana, sighing on moonlit nights, and the girl in the transparent long dress, barefoot on a Pacific beach, strumming a guitar and languorously singing, here is Walt of the amazing prickette.

—Oh, come on, Poker!

—Come, dear daughters of Texas and sweet angels of Louisiana, here is Walt of the withered sackettes.

—Aw, Poker!

—Fat, overfed slob!

—Who gave me fourteen ounce steaks for dinner, who gave me double helpings of cheese cake and pecan pie and chocolate ice cream? Who gave me a fifth of whiskey every other day and a case of beer to drink with a game of cards? Who sat me down in the Lay-Z-Boy in front of the TV to watch pro football and kept bringing me popcorn and tortilla chips and Coke? What do you want me to do now, for god's sake, take a vacation in Bangla Desh?

A call came through from the sheriff's office informing me of the cattle rustlers in the Panhandle. The office had been working on the case for several months, slowly accumulating clues. It was now established that the operation was run from Abilene by Fingers Dawson.

—What do you have on Fingers? I asked.

—Six foot two, the sheriff replied, hundred and eighty pounds, Cauc, normal features, red hair that you can see from a mile.

—Okay.

—Okay, replied the sheriff, giving more information. Size ten shoes, forty-two waist, shirt collar sixteen and a half. Sings when he's doin' nuthin'. Good baritone voice. Taps his fingers together when he sings.

26

—Okay. Any examples?

—Okay. Ballads mostly. Makes 'em up while lounging in the beer garden, though he's never been seen with a guitar. Okay, here's an example:

> Suzy Jane of Abilene
> You're the prettiest gal I ever seen
> Let me take you to the pastures, Suzy Jane,
> And let me show you what I mean.

—Okay, I said.

—Okay, replied the sheriff, not much of a goddamn ballad, is it?

—Okay, I said. Something like this one?

> Down by the china-berry
> I feel O very-very
> Under the spreading mimosa
> Let me come closer.

—Yeah, that kinda crap, the sheriff said. This one's more like it:

> I loved her in the Plaza
> And I loved her in the Waldorf
> But when I lost all my money
> The romance was called orf.

—Okay, I said, I'm on my way.

—Okay, the sheriff said, hanging up.

I walked across the room and took a bottle of beer from the icebox. I went and sat in a rocking chair in the corner of the room and began reading a magazine that told you how to make home improvements. Poker came over with some tortilla chips and a bowl of cheese dip she'd been making while I was on the phone.

—Thought you'd like to snack, she said, placing the chips and the dip on a small table beside the rocking chair and herself sitting down opposite me and beginning to crochet a shawl.

—Thanks, Poker, I said, sipping the beer.

—Before you ride out to Abilene, she said.

—I was thinking maybe we could pull down the wall between the spare bedrooms, make French doors out to the garden and pave the area that's now overrun by weeds. We could have a den and a neat little sitting area outside.

—You fixing to do that now? Poker asked.

—Aw, it's only an idea I've had, I said. We could pick up some bricks cheap for the paving, there's an old brick house on Twenty-third they're knocking down to build an apartment complex and I was talking to the foreman the other day and he said Sure you can have the bricks a dime apiece, and I asked him, You sure you don't need them for the apartments, and he said, Mister, we're using the best stone veneer for the facing to get the right country effect and we don't need no bricks, it's to be called, he added in a confidential whisper, Tudor Rose Villas. Why, I said, that's swell, and we shook on it.

—The bricks will do fine, Poker said. I'd pave the area in circles around the purple sage, and maybe we could plant a live-oak for shade.

—That's what I'd figured, too, I said.

—I don't suppose you plan going to Abilene, Poker said.

—I'm waiting for a call from the sheriff, I said.

—But you just had one!

—That wasn't the sheriff, I said. That was a trap by one of Fingers Dawson's men. The voice nearly fooled me though. I could've sworn it was the sheriff. But when he got on to the ballad I became suspicious. Uh-huh, I said to myself, there's something phoney here.

—What do you mean?

—Sloppy rhyming, I thought to myself, I said. Fingers, I thought, is a professional with the fastest draw this side of Dodge City, he's not going to ruin his reputation with that kind of a ballad. So I made up one to test the caller and when he agreed I knew for certain.

—Go on, finish the tortilla chips, I got some more, Poker said.

—And another thing, I said. The sheriff has a poor memory. He said to me last night when we were sitting outside the county jail, smoking a pipe and talking about improving real estate values by getting the Santa Fe railroad to construct a line to here, Walt, he said, I have the poorest goddamn memory a man was ever cursed with. Now here we are talking about the Santa Fe railroad, he said, and I know for sure that when I meet Wes Turner tomorrow to hear about the corn prices, Wes, I'm going to say, I was sitting right here last night with what's his name, ah yes, Walt, I was sitting right here with Walt talking about bringing a railroad to town and I'm damned if I can remember which railroad we were talking of, maybe it was the Penn Central, maybe it was Southern Pacific, and that's what I told Walt last night, Walt, I told him, I'm going to forget by tomorrow when I talk to Wes that we've been talking about the Santa Fe railroad, that's how it is with me, Wes, and, Walt, that's how it is. That's how the sheriff is, I said to Poker, he can't remember two words, how could he remember four lines of a ballad?

—Wouldn't Fingers Dawson know that, about the sheriff's memory?

—He knows about it all right, I said.

—Then why would his man quote four lines of a ballad if he knew the sheriff would be incapable of it?

—Because he knows that I know, that's why, I said.

—Ah, Poker said, that figures. Let me get you another beer.

—Poker, I said, when she'd brought me the beer, we should make a list of the things we need for the den. Shag carpet, I was thinking.

—You going to make a barbecue pit out by the patio, too?

—I have many plans to improve the place.

—Sure, she said.

I sprang out of the rocking chair, ran to the hallway where four guns were placed in a rack, took two of them, ran back to the window of the front room and crouched beside it, placing one gun on the floor. I had heard riders in the west and now saw a small funnel cloud of dust on the horizon spiralling closer to the house and growing larger each moment. The thudding of the horses on the hard, dry land grew louder, too.

The dusty land seemed to float in the white, shimmering heat as if it had detached itself from the earth and had commenced to levitate toward some other sphere. The spiralling cloud had grown so large that although the riders were still a hundred yards away the air was already charged with dust. My nostrils twitched, I could see minute flecks of dust settle on my sweating arms, subtly changing the color of my skin. I realized that in the apprehension and the heat my mouth had been open, for my lower lip had become coated with dust and a lump had developed in my throat. In that moment in which one surrenders himself to totally inappropriate and irrelevant thoughts in a situation fraught with danger it occurred to me that were I to remove my knee-high boots and the thick socks that I'd bought at the Army and Navy store there'd be dust between my toes, that were I to stand under a shower the tub would fill up with dust pouring down my armpits and my chest and my groin, from behind my ears and from out of every pore of my skin. During that same moment I remembered the last time I'd met Jerry Shuberg in New York when he'd said, Remember, Walt, the land gets under your skin in the West.

The riders were now close enough to be discerned as individuals. I relaxed my grip on the gun seeing that the group was led by Archie Mozzer and Scott Bixler who were firing their guns in the air, laughing and shouting, followed by the boys, all riding toward the Saturday night dream that beginning with the sting of whiskey in the throat and reaching for the satin-gowned apparition that beckons down hallways must inevitably end with the tongue gone swollen in a sour mouth.

Reversals, the thwarted anticipations, the loss of intensity. With such knowledge, still the riding into town, the bright-eyed expectations, always the naïveté of renewed desires: always the conviction of a new America.

I put the gun on my shoulder and walked back to where I'd tied Gary to a cedar tree. I'd spent the morning following deer trails but a couple of squirrels and a cottonmouth moccasin coiling up a Spanish-oak were all the life I'd seen. The forest was dense and secretive, its trees a conspiracy of silence and watchfulness. I'd come to this land before, many times; I'd sat by the water's edge where a deer-track ended, waiting at sunrise by the still water; I'd penetrated darknesses with a wildly beating heart. I'd interpreted passages of time; I'd structured hypotheses in my mind, I'd put light and shadow together so that the explanation might diminish the terrors of the deadly quiet forest. I figured I was ready to take on the inevitable desert, I was ready for high noon on the sands a thousand miles from the nearest tree.

I'd just mounted Gary and was thinking about the princess I was destined to meet when something made me look behind me at the cliff a quarter of a mile away to my rear. A figure on horseback was watching me. From that distance, I could distinguish only the outline but was convinced I saw a drooping moustache. He flicked the reins and turned his horse back, seeing that I'd observed him, and as he turned around to ride away, I thought I clearly saw the sun catch the color and texture of his face: it was not red but pink and was marked by purple splotches. I didn't reckon I could catch up with him even if Gary galloped twice the speed of his horse and so I shouted to the sky above me, with no hope of being heard, You can't stop me now, old tormentor! I will see the princess. I shall cross the desert and find her even if I have only my own bones to lay at her feet. I shall enter the brightest daylight, the dazzling high noon of the desert.

Entry and withdrawal, considerations of ideas and the subsequent finality of the shoulders dismissively shrugging away obvious improbabilities. Ah, well, there's always revision.

—Hortense, I whispered, walking down the hall and standing beneath the glittering chandelier. She appeared at the top of the wide, curving staircase and stood looking silently down at me for a moment before taking slow, deliberate steps down the staircase. She wore a white gown and white satin shoes. Her black hair hung straight down to the small of her back. Her cheeks were a pale white, her eyes a bright black and glinting with a thousand reflections of the chandelier, and her teeth too, with the lips held slightly open, radiated the sparkling light.

—Poker Hortense, I whispered, awed by her magnificent presence, seeing the turquoise and silver necklace at her bosom. She was tall from my point of view, so that I could see only parts of her at a time. I walked to the foot of the staircase when she was half-way down. There were roundnesses to her body, voluptuous amplitudes. There was the swelling of oceans within her, the loneliness of mountain peaks. I could not look anywhere and not see her. She stopped when she was three or four steps from the bottom. There was a whiteness surrounding me, distances of blinding perspective. I dropped down upon a knee and bowed my head.

O Nights that brought me to her body bare!

III

Notes for Hulme on Sexual Symptoms

Maybe it was Oklahoma or Kansas or even the Texas Panhandle; certainly, it was in the middle of the country and to the south of it. We had been driving southwest in the Buick station-wagon with the fake mahogany finish on its exterior, nosing down after St Louis toward New Mexico. After a picnic lunch of devilled eggs, roast beef sandwiches, a wedge of pecan pie, and two cans of Bud, I'd dozed off in the rear seat, taking some time to overcome my repugnance for the abrasive texture of the vinyl upholstery which looked like soft leather before I fell asleep. With the radio playing some country music and the air conditioning turned up, Rosemary settled down to seventy miles an hour on the interstate highway. I listened to the music for a while finding its repetitive rhythms and banal lyrics a decided help in going to sleep, and was particularly struck by the silliness of one which went

Ah'm a country boy from Kansas
Ah'm the all American male
Ah love you like ah love the prairie
Mah love for you will never fail

which was not only an empty boast but which was also cynical, being rendered by a teenage Jew who had never left Brooklyn.

When I awoke, the radio was still playing but the car had come to a stop. I pushed myself up on my elbows and saw that Rosemary had gone out, leaving her door open so that the buzzer sounded irritably to remind her that she had left the key behind. I reached up and pulled the key out and saw that Rosemary was standing in front and looking down at the car, her hands on her hips. I thought maybe we'd had a flat and rose, with some effort, out of my seat and went out, saying Jesus!

The object of Rosemary's curiosity was a turtle which was wearily determined to traverse the distance between the left wheel and the right wheel and had hit upon the notion that the shortest distance followed a slightly diagonal path.

—O for god's sake! I said, looking up past the hood to see that the windshield was flecked with smashed insects as if it had been bespattered with bird-droppings.

—I stopped to stretch my legs, that's all, Rosemary said, turning around to look westward where the sun was not far from the horizon. There was a talk show on the radio, she went on, a guy called Charles Heams or something was saying that nature is a copy of art.

—Bullshit! I said.

—Your only comment at the time was to snore, she said.

—Quite appropriate too, I said.

—Not that it is, Heams said, for we can never know what it is, but what we observe of it, and what we observe of it is determined by what we've learned to observe in art—a landscape is as pretty as a picture. This is true even for the uninstructed among us, for it has become a common gesture to suppress one's ignorance simply by positing that, of course, there's a lot more there than the row of elms receding to the horizon.

—Look about you, I said, and that is when I first noticed that we were surrounded by wheat that grew as high as our shoulders, so that I said, Jesus, where are we?

—Just off the highway, Rosemary said. I told you I wanted to stretch my legs, there was no rest area the last fifty miles, and I thought instead of driving on until one came I'd just go off the highway for a while.

—But, Rosemary, there's no road here.

—Sure, there's no road here, I can see that.

—You mean to say you plowed right through the wheat?

—There was a track.

—What do you mean there was? Where's it gone now?

She had no answer. I jumped on the hood to see if I could get any kind of a view of the situation from there, for from the ground nothing was to be seen past the high wheat that surrounded us.

From the hood, too, I saw only the wheat growing around us, and so climbed up on the roof of the car, thinking, Jesus, what a land! From the roof, I could see for maybe twenty miles in every direction. The land was flat and covered with wheat. No path led to where we were, I saw no highway in the distance nor heard the sound of traffic. The wheat grew so close to the car that I wondered how we had opened the doors. There were shoots of wheat growing in the gaps between the bumpers and the body of the car, and it seemed as if the car had been abandoned in the wheatfield a long time ago and that a whole new crop had grown around it.

—What is this? I asked. Rosemary, where have you brought me?

Just then I saw in the distance a combine cutting a wide path through the wheat, and feeling less agitated on seeing the farmer at his labor, I came down from the roof of the car. The sun must have set when I was on the roof for now it had grown quite dark, which I thought was strange since I only just now saw the farmer in full daylight, but I didn't look for an explanation, having discovered many years ago the futility of so doing: what happens happens and I can only have a memory of it, and luckily I'm blessed with a good memory.

I could not see Rosemary and waited silently for a few minutes, thinking that she had probably gone about some natural business. I leaned back against the car and breathed in the cool night air, noticing that stars had appeared in the sky. A breeze had risen and the wheat swayed in it. Rosemary did not return. I called her name, softly at first, once or twice, and then loudly several times. What's the matter, Rosemary, I yelled, got diarrhea or something? I heard music and hands clapping and, thinking that the car radio was still on, playing some more lousy country western, reached in through the window to switch it off, but discovered that it was already off. I called Rosemary again. Someone clapped loudly over a general muffled sound of clapping. I looked in that direction which was to the rear of the car. Not twenty yards away on the square back yard of a two-storeyed house, under the colored lights that had been fixed up in the trees, there was a crowd of people dancing, Rosemary among them.

Colorful skirts were swirling above the close-cut grass of the lawn, long blond hair trailed through the air, lipsticked mouths floated in the night. Audacities played in the eyes, abandon in the teeth, picking up intensities of light. Bare white arms rose and fell, bosoms swelled. The music came from the ground, ejecting its vibrations from between blades of grass, waves of it penetrating calf and thigh muscles and charging them with a patterned mobility.

I went and stood under a live-oak behind a bench where two elderly men sat watching the dancing. I was surprised to see how easily Rosemary had become one of the group. She bore herself with the same confident composure as the native girls as if she too had long waited for this night with keen anticipations of the heart, as if she had been attuning herself, sitting on close, languorous afternoons in front of the mirror brushing her hair, for present fulfilments. As if she too had walked down the steps of the back porch of the two-storeyed house, raising her skirt and throwing a glance at the tall men come from the harvesting.

The wheat was in and the men who had seen from their harvesters the shadows of the swiftly floating clouds cast momentary depressions over the land, whose eyes had followed the waves of wind swelling the wheat into a billowing mass, who had been alone with the sun and the earth, had scrubbed the dust from their armpits and groins, washed the horizons from their eyes, had come to the night's softnesses, beer chilling their throats, promises warm in their hearts.

The two men on the bench in front of me had been talking but I had not heard them until now.

—Come on, Charlie, one was saying, you didn't spend all afternoon at the barber's to come and sit here, you can do it, too.

—I could too, Charlie said, but I like to watch the youngsters, it's their turn now.

—Sure, Charlie, the other said. You been around, too, down in the Keys with the ocean whispering over the moonlit surface, tropical breezes blowing straight from Cuba, I seen you lie there under the palm trees with Mary Lou, her skirt thrown back, the moonlight casting a clean shadow on her raised legs, your mouth at her moveables, marvelling at softnesses, loving it when she

36

lets out a sharp little suppressed scream, sure, Charlie, you been around.

—Quit remindin' me, will you, Joe!

—And in Alabama in the cottonfield, right in the middle of the afternoon, ripping the soiled blouse off the black girl you'd seen walking down the path, a basket of cotton on her head, her arms lifted to the basket, her armpits black with sweat, and you pulled her down right there by you, going crazy seeing the sweat pour down her neck in rivulets and rise up the slopes of her breasts like rivers flowing back to their source and you went straight for the source, Charlie, you drank up the sweat there, where it collected, you'd gone crazy with the smell of the sun and the earth that had become distilled in the sweat, you sucked at the little concavity at the base of her throat, you held her arms back and sucked at her armpits, drawing her wet hair into your mouth, you pulled her skirt down and drove your lips across the insides of her thighs where the sweat was flowing, wildly you drove your tongue right into her, your hardened tongue sought her interior wetnesses, you were crazy with that smell.

—Oh, come on, Joe!

—And in Maine with the big-boned Miss Elizabeth Markham in the pine woods, her jolly laughter as though she were at a polo match, her pure-bred fragrance more potent to your senses than the pine in the air, all the pine in Maine, Charlie, and the way she pretended she had no notion of what you were up to, that drove you wild, eh, Charlie? Come on now, what artful fuckery were you up to in the pine woods in Maine?

—Come on, Joe, quit remindin' me!

—Elsie, remember Elsie in the industrial wasteland of Newark, at the back of the railroad tracks on a bed of trash surrounded by heaped up aluminum cans, rusting contortions of ironwork and all the shitification that no rainfall is ever going to wash away? You were there, Charlie, fat, slobbering, clumsy Elsie underneath you, garbage-fleshed ungainly Elsie with pudgy arms and swollen cheeks, her twisted mouth panting in little grunts, her hair thick and matted and lice-ridden, that was okay with you, loverboy, your mouth falling off her rubbery dangler and grasping some

37

turdette in all that trash was okay, too, in that putrid air under the sky black with soot.

—I was young then, Joe, I had to take what I could get, I had desires then.

—You went west, Charlie, the frontier was wide open, there were easy conquests to be had to satisfy your craving, you'd had enough of riding through the streets of Boston in your brougham, suffocating in your morning coat and top hat, you rode west looking for the security and the terror, the peace and the turbulence that only the prairie could give you.

Charlie was shaking his head as if in disbelief of his former accomplishments. I moved away from under the tree and walked toward the house. A little distance away from the bench, I looked back and saw Charlie's face for the first time. He had fat, swollen cheeks, so that his eyes appeared to be sunken and tiny. His lips were so thin as to be no more than a line below the nose. His chin appeared to be small, having successive folds of flesh hanging from it, so that he did not seem to possess a neck. His open-neck shirt was tight at the armpits and loose at the chest and stretched taut at the stomach where the buttons were on the point of coming off. Just as I was observing him, he rose with Joe's help for his considerable bulk had taken from him the independence of movement. Having risen from the bench, he took slow steps toward the house. His stomach appeared vaster than before, his trousers having that spaciousness about them which indicates that most of the material has gone into encircling the waist. I stood beside the potted geraniums that were placed in a circle around a tree on a paved area outside the porch, and saw Charlie laboriously drag himself toward the steps to the porch. He seemed to pause for a brief moment with each step and to take a deep breath as if preparatory to an overwhelming labor and, with a painful grimace on his face, push himself forward. When he reached the steps, he first held the railing with both his hands as if he were about to tear it away from the house and then pulled himself up to the first step, pausing to tug at the railing before each subsequent step. There were only four steps up to the porch, but it took Charlie nearly five minutes to climb them. On accomplishing his ascent, he appeared to be so relieved that he gave a boyish little hop of delight; in doing so, he lost his balance and staggered forward, wildly flailing his arms in order to grasp something; his left hand got hold of the table-cloth that covered the long table which had upon it bottles of liquor, plastic glasses, paper plates, plastic knives and forks, a vast ham, several kinds of dip, plates full of potato chips, and some paper napkins. Charlie, staggering still, held on to the cloth while his knees gave way. He crashed against the floor, dragging the cloth with him, and all the contents of the table went scattering all over the floor, the bottles shattering, the ham thudding against the pine boards, all simultaneously. In a moment there was a crowd of people on the porch expressing concern, sympathy, consternation, anger, despair, kindness, hatred, some called out Charlie!, some shouting Good God! across the lawn, some Jesus!, and some Shit! Finally, Charlie was helped on to his feet and slowly walked back to his bench in the garden and given three bottles of beer and a sack full of potato chips.

A new checkered cloth was spread across the table and fresh provisions laid out upon it. The long-skirted ladies busied themselves arranging the table neatly and clearing away what had fallen on the floor. Within five minutes, Charlie was on to his second bottle of beer, had accepted the offer of a charcoal-broiled steak with baked potatoes and cole slaw, the ladies had returned to the dancing, the music played more gaily than before, and the few cowboys who stood around under the trees had lit cigarettes and were laughing at one another's jokes. Old Glory which had been hanging limply high upon its mast began to flutter a little now that a soft breeze had arisen from the south.

I walked up to the table on the porch and helped myself to a couple of crackers and was debating whether I should cut myself a slice of roast beef or eat instead a small plate of potato salad, or both with a slice of rye bread, when I saw across the porch, just past the railing, a figure I thought I recognized. My hand was suspended over the knife that lay next to the beef. I withdrew it, softly munched the cracker in my mouth, put my hand to my hip, and in that frozen position cast a sideways glance at the figure who stood in the shadow. I quietly took a few steps back until my back was to the wall. From there, I took slow, soft steps sideways along the wall until I had reached the railing while the figure, who faced the dancing and therefore was turned away from me, was some five feet away on the other side of the railing and in a shadow which was cast by the pitch of the roof. I waited and thought I could hear some words. I leaned over the railing and strained to distinguish the words from all the noise of the music and the laughter. It was a ballad, and finally I made out one of the verses to be:

> Ah bin ridin' thru Tayksus,
> Thru Wyomin' and Califona,
> Ah never seed a gal who could
> Compare with mah Ramona.

I noticed, too, that he had his hands behind him and that he was tapping the fingers together, beating out the rhythm of the ballad. It never crossed my mind that it would be implausible for Fingers Dawson to have a girl called Ramona and therefore I did not suspect the authenticity of the verse; I guess seeing the fingers hitting each other so emphatically just about sent the blood pumping to my head and I was on the point of leaping over the railing, holding my gun to Fingers Dawson's back and saying, Okay, Fingers, cut the goddamn ballad, I'm taking you in for rustling cattle in the Panhandle, when he turned around as if pivoting on one heel, his gun flashing. In the same moment, I had my gun out, too, and I must have fired a fraction of a second after he did. I guess neither of us was aiming to kill the other, for at such short range you'd have to be an armadillo with a water-pistol to miss. His shot went over my left shoulder and crashed into the cedar boarding of the back wall while my shot splintered the rock beside his left boot. And even as the shots were being fired, Fingers had begun to run and I had jumped over the railing in pursuit of him. He ran straight into the dancers where he figured I wouldn't fire. I ran after him, found myself momentarily trapped among the swirling dancers and being blinded by the vivid greens and pinks of the women's low-cut dresses which appeared to fling their uplifted, white-skinned orbulets at me in maddening flashes, and then out of the crowd across a field and into a barn.

I approached the barn gingerly, knowing that Fingers was already there. I pushed the door without going in. The door creaked slowly. Nothing happened. Fingers knew about these tricks, and he wasn't going to fire at empty space. You had to be dumb to fire at a moving hat or where you figured a shadow was coming from. There was a light inside the barn, maybe from a hurricane lamp, and I guessed that Fingers must already be positioned where I wouldn't see him while he'd have me in the open light. I walked to the back of the barn, ducking under the windows as I walked. There was a ladder placed against a window on the second storey. I slowly climbed up it, my gun in hand. I took it easy raising myself at the window, making no more sound than a snake that's eaten a nestful of bird's eggs and is fast asleep. I climbed in at the window and lowered myself slowly on to the floor. It was easy to make no noise since the floor was ankle-deep in hay; it was some forty feet wide and another thirty long before it ended, falling to the lower floor with only a ladder on the side of the wall to connect the two floors. Fingers hadn't observed me; at least he hadn't fired. I guessed he was still watching the door downstairs. Just then I heard a sound that almost made me fire into the darkness before I realized it was a woman's voice. All it said was O Jimmy! It was said in the tone a woman uses when she's being made love to and she likes it the way it's made. A little light reached up from where Fingers had placed the lamp on the lower floor, and soon I distinguished a couple in the far corner of the floor where I was, making love. I just sat down right where I was since I didn't want to disturb the lovers or retreat the way I had come. I wondered what Fingers was thinking about, but as I began to see more in that very dim light my attention was drawn to the couple in the corner. Now, let me say that I don't care to be a spectator at someone else's love-making; if there's to be any love-making I prefer it to be my own. Why, once in a saloon in Denver a barkeeper whispered in my ear that for five dollars he could arrange for me to see a show of two girls doing extraordinary things, as he phrased it, to each other, and I said to him, Mister, that ain't my idea of pleasure and I don't care for no show, but here's ten dollars and I'd be delighted to do astonishingly extraordinary things to both the ladies, one at a time, in succession, and with no goddamn spectators around. So, I wasn't interested in what was happening in the corner, especially as my mind was more on what Fingers was thinking of down below. But maybe I was getting bored with just waiting or maybe common human curiosity got the better of me; in any case, there was nothing else there to do, and so I took a passing glance and then another to see if what I thought I'd seen was in fact happening. The lovers had removed their clothes, which was natural enough, considering it was a warm night and you could see stars through the window, and who wouldn't have done the same under the circumstances? But Jimmy, who appeared to be a little old for assignations in a barn—maybe that was only a trick of the light and he was no more than twenty, but his stomach was like a watermelon already—this Jimmy had a belt at his waist with a gun on it. What made Jimmy's stomach so obviously visible was that he appeared to be sitting astride the girl's chest who lay on her back with some extra hay under her head as a kind of a pillow, and in that position his belly had a blown, distended look to it. As I began to see what was going on, I saw that Jimmy wasn't exactly sitting on the girl, he was somehow suspended over her, his feet on either side of her shoulders, his hands on his knees so that his buttocks hung above the girl's breast without touching her. Well, this was okay, too, everyone to his own goddamn thrill, I said to myself, when I saw the precise nature of Jimmy's excitement. He had turned the belt around so that the gun could dangle from between his thighs, and it was the barrel of the gun that the girl had in her hand and which she again and again inserted into her mouth, saying O Jimmy! whenever she withdrew it. This really got my curiosity excited and I stared as hard as I could. A little later, Jimmy shuffled his large body, holding the gun close to his thighs, and lay flat upon the girl, compressing his stomach against hers so that much of his loose flesh seemed to fall out at the sides. He lay there for a few minutes, rocking with increasing momentum. Then suddenly he pulled his hand out, stretched out his arm, waving the gun in the air, and fired three shots in quick succession. His body seemed to become totally exhausted after he had fired the shots and he fell to the side of the girl. She, too, appeared to sink into a swoon.

I had no time to work out what my adversary below thought of the sexual fireworks, for just as I watched Jimmy drop off on to the girl's side and was about to give a closer scrutiny to the girl to see what kind of a female would permit what I had just witnessed, at that moment I saw what looked like a flare or a ball of fire, I was not sure precisely what in that instant, describe a neat parabola through the air and land right beside me. It was a hurricane lamp, I noticed the moment it landed, and I figured that Fingers had hurled it up in order to set the barn on fire and to have me roasted alive. As it happened, however, the lamp landed on its base and did not tip over; the chimney smoked for a second, the flame rose as if it wanted to get right out of the lamp and take over the hay and then reduced itself to the level of the wick and, a moment later, died. I had seen a shadowy figure below just at the moment after the lamp had been hurled and in that moment I had fired two shots in its direction. There was silence below but, on hearing the shots, the girl in the corner had sighed O Jimmy! No doubt she had her arm endearingly across Jimmy and gave his face a tender little pat, for he grunted most contentedly in response. I crept silently toward the ladder to the lower floor and began to descend slowly, feeling my way down, step by step. I must have been some four or five feet from the ground when I realized that a rung was missing from the ladder. My foot was very near the wall and as I moved it as far down as I could and found nothing there and then drew it back up again before deciding whether or not to jump off the ladder, I flicked, in the process, with my foot, a switch on the wall and the lights came on in the barn. My reaction was immediately to jump off and to dive for cover behind some farm machinery, for in that moment of the lights coming on Fingers fired a shot that blasted a hole two inches away from the switch; and while I was making my dive for cover, I managed a shot that narrowly missed his left ear whereas he, in that very instant, seeing that I had escaped his shot and instead had nearly blown his head apart, ran out of the door. I ran to the door and stood just inside it. While I was standing there, I happened to look upon the ground where Fingers had left his footprints in the sawdust. It took me a few moments to realize the significance of the footprints: they could not possibly be those of Fingers Dawson and I began to think, too, of the absurdity of the Califona-Ramona rhyme. The man who had just run out had small feet, his shoe size was maybe seven, certainly no larger than eight. Fingers Dawson, as every law officer in the land knew, wore size ten.

There was no sound outside and I walked out of the barn. The day had dawned, a red cardinal was singing on the top of a live-oak from where, looking east, he would have seen a horizon the same color as his feathers, several cocks were crowing, and Dan in his dirty overalls was walking across the muddy ground on his way to feeding the pigs. I began to walk away but, on hearing some sound at a window, paused and stood under a tree.

It was the same window that I had climbed into during the night. A large, heavy man with flabby, flaccid tissues of flesh banded together to form his body, entirely naked except for a belt and a gun at his waist, had begun to descend down the ladder. In the dark I had not been able to guess his age; he appeared now to be about forty as he laboriously made his way down the ladder, his feet trembling in the air each time they groped for the next rung. When he was half-way, the ladder seemed to become bent like a bow under his weight. At that moment, the girl appeared at the window.

By contrast to Jimmy, she was dressed from head to foot in a gown of a white transparent material. I could not see her face since she was turned to the wall while she descended. She came down very slowly, her white satin shoes emerging from her long dress and being tentatively suspended for a moment before finding a step each time she lowered herself. Jimmy, reaching the ground, held the ladder while the girl came down and when she, too, had reached the ground, she put her arms around Jimmy's shoulders and he picked her up as if he were about to carry her across a threshold. It was at that moment that I saw her face.

It was the ancient, ageless face of a woman who had passed her eightieth year so long ago that she no longer could tell her age. Jimmy walked away slowly, carrying her light body, her dress trailing down. He reached a river and began to ford it, stepping on stones that had been put there to make a path. Half-way in the river, he lowered himself and placed the woman upon the water which was shallow enough at this point for the woman to rest on the river-bed without being entirely submerged in the water. Jimmy rose, and walked across the river, climbed up the bank and continued to walk toward the swamp in the west. I hurried to the river, wondering whether I were not a witness to a homicide; for all I knew, Jimmy could have drugged the woman or knocked her out before depositing her in the river. By the time I reached there, the level of the water had risen.

When I stepped upon the stones which Jimmy had used to walk across the river, I found the water come up to my chest. I persevered, however, and waded in as far as the point where Jimmy had placed the woman in the water. By now the water was reaching my chin. It was clear, transparent water as if the snows had just melted of which it was composed. There, in the center of the river, I saw her body, but only for a moment.

The white dress seemed to have dissolved away and almost as if the water had some magical power, her body had become transformed to a woman no older than twenty. I could not tell whether she was living or dead. There was a smile upon her lips and a certain sparkle in her eyes and her hands seemed to move like an underwater swimmer's although her body did not move but remained suspended in the water, neither lying heavily upon the bottom nor floating on the surface. It was a vision both intensely beautiful and awfully terrifying.

A moment later, however, the water began to become muddy as if an undercurrent were loosening the silt. Soon the transparency of the water was all gone. The water was thick and turned from brown to black, losing its fluidity, its luminosity. It began to smell. First faintly as if gas were escaping in a room and one could not locate the leak. Then the smell became stronger and turned into an unbearable stench.

IV

The Elimination of the Mexican Woman

I turned back from the river, walked down two blocks, turned left, westward, for a block to where the El Dorado Motel stood on the corner of Second and Washington. It was a brand new motel, part of the Bodenstein chain that was maintaining a healthy spot on Wall Street at a time when all else needed to be evacuated to a sanatorium, and faced the Torres Brothers supermarket (with the cartoon sign outside it of the two brothers outlined in neon, grinning idiotically at each other) next to which was the barber shop run by Harry Kateusz who was popularly and affectionately known in the town as the Shears.

Earlier, I'd spent an hour at Harry's getting a shave and a face massage. Harry's clean hands with neatly clipped fingernails deftly worked about my face for ten minutes, and I was through; the best part of the hour, however, I'd waited my turn, glancing at magazines which showed naked girls in full bloom walking across gardens of azaleas, roses and fountains, or naked girls leaning out of windows beside which morning-glory climbed in a purple riot, breathing in the fresh morning air, or naked girls lying beside the tire-marks upon a sand-dune. Enough to make a guy want to thank his lucky stars and stripes for democracy and freedom of fantastic thought. But though I looked about for clues in the barber shop (while my eyes seemed intent upon penetrating the colorful pages and while such idle thoughts as they ought to keep horror stories in barber shops to make the customer's hair stand on end occurred to me in passing) I observed none. Sure, the Shears talked a great deal as he snipped the hour away, but his monologue consisted mainly of lamenting the late untimely floods which had turned the cotton-growers' expected record profit into a twenty million dollar loss and had led to the Governor sending a telegram to the President, asking for the region to be declared a disaster area. Well, we all knew this from the TV news, but still it was dramatic the way the Shears told the story. When it was my turn, the Shears greeted me with, And how are you today?, and proceeded immediately to shave my face and to continue his monologue, ignoring my response that I was okay and would have been better had not the brand new plumbing of the El Dorado motel intimidated my bowels, for shining chrome plain turns me off. So, there was nothing here, I was saying to myself and wondering why Jerry Biderman had said when I was flying out of Washington, D.C., Have a look at the barber shop run by Harry Kateusz, they call him the Shears, when, my face being tapped gently by the barber's soft fingers, I saw a cat jump up to the counter in front of the mirror, balance itself among several jars and tubes of lotions and hair tonics and sprays, sit down in a very small area without disturbing any of the items there and, raising a hindleg from a squatting position, begin to lick its genitals. Look at that, the Shears said, licking his goddamn balls as if they were his paws, casual as hell, not even tickled by the experience: boy, I tell you if men could do that, massage parlors would go out of business. It was a pretty cat, a Siamese, but I saw no significance either in the cat nor in the comments upon it by the Shears until much later, until when I was walking back from the river and entering the El Dorado motel. Just at the door, I glanced back across the road, saw the barber shop and noticed that the cat was just outside the shop, looking up at the candy-pole. Suddenly, another statement of Jerry Biderman's came back to me as I walked into the motel, flashed a smile to Dolores, the receptionist, and took the elevator to the twentieth floor in order to get to the roof. There are two connections, Jerry Biderman had said, and we think they're very near the top; one is called the Cat. That's simple enough, Jerry went on, for what can be simpler than letting everyone in town call Harry Kateusz the Shears and to call him the Cat in the underworld, but the other one's known as Mesa—M.E.S.A. You crack that one, Walt, and win yourself a weekend in Vegas for two. I was watching the floor numbers flash rapidly as the elevator silently went up, hearing Jerry's words and thinking to myself: The Cat. The Siamese Cat. Siamese. Mese. Mesa. It was a logical progression. The Cat and Mesa were one and the same, Harry Kateusz, the Shears. I got out on the twentieth floor, went past the door of the Restaurant of Two Nations where you could eat hamburgers and look at Mexico or eat enchiladas and look at the U.S. or work on the quiz printed on paper napkins with such brain-twisters as The Alamo is in . . . (check one) San Francisco, San Antonio, San Diego. I went past it with last night's memory of Steak à la Pancho Villa with New Yorker French fries, and climbed up a stone staircase and stepped out on the roof. From there I could see the Customs checkpoint on the river where a long line of cars and trucks was very slowly coming up the bridge and crowds of people walking across the frontier, shopping bags in hand.

I observed the scene through a pair of binoculars, watched the automobiles, pickups, VW wagons, and trucks drive up to the checkpoint and be examined. I took out my pipe from my pocket, filled it with a mixture I'd prepared in my tobacco pouch of Granger and Latakia, two-thirds and a third respectively, which made it a very pleasant smoke though I wasn't a serious smoker, but one has to do these things professionally, and lit the pipe. As soon as the flame touched the tobacco, the transmitter embedded in the briar was automatically activated, and taking a puff, I said, the pipe still in my mouth, Okay, Donnelly, I'm with you and I think I know which road the mule's going to take.

A ring of smoke popped up from the pipe and hung before my eyes before dissipating itself, and Donnelly's voice came over: Oh, hi there, Walt, did the Shears give you a good shave?

—Sure, I said, it was pretty close.

—Did you go to the beach? Donnelly asked. It sure was a good day for it yesterday. The missis took the kids over and they had a swell time.

—I'm glad to hear that, I said. How's the traffic?

—It's okay, Donnelly said. Hey, what do you know, my boy Chris took a boat out and caught a couple of red snappers, how about that, eh? They cooked 'em right there on the beach, fixed some French fries and had a heck of a time.

—Listen, Donnelly, your guys let that VW wagon past pretty quickly.

—Sure, he said, everyone knows we suspect long-haired guys in VW wagons, but the truth is we don't since they all know we suspect 'em and therefore stay clean or clear of VW wagons, 'sides it's mainly university professors going across to eat cabrito for god's sake or maybe to pick up cheap antiques. I'm blowed if I know what's wrong with American antiques, we make 'em like the best in the world.

—What about that Dodge pickup? I asked.

—I see it, Donnelly said. Pretty good for a '69 model, not a dent in it, maybe the guy uses it only for visiting the whorehouse and employs mules on his ranch, the world is full of weirdos, Walt.

—Talking of mules, Donnelly, are you watching for the one we expect today?

—Sure, Walt, all the men are out there, as you can see.

—Shit, Donnelly, Washington's breathing down my neck, we can't miss this one.

—Careful, Walt, you'll get a red neck that way, ha, ha!

—Oh, come on, Donnelly!

—Say, why don't you call me Chris?

—Okay, Chris, let's not miss anything, okay?

—Sure, I'm watching everything, I can even see you had a close shave, your chin's shining like a baby's ass. By the way, did you notice anything at the barber's?

—No, what should I have noticed?

—You're the expert, Walt.

—Okay, so what should I have noticed?

—Harry Kateusz is a pretty good barber, he talks all the time you'd think he was no more than the Shears.

—What do you mean, Chris?

—Oh, come on, you've heard of the Cat and of Mesa.

—You know those names!

—Sure, who doesn't? he said. Ask that dame at the receptionist's desk at the El Dorado, you know the one I mean, odorous Dolores, shit I can smell her cunt from here! Ask her, if you can stop from going mad in her presence, where you can find the Cat, and she'll point to the establishment of Mr. Harry Kateusz across the road.

—What if I asked her for Mesa?

—Ah, she'll shrug her shoulders and you'd get a mighty fine view of her rippling nipplers, what else can you ask for in this life, eh, Walt? What a smell though, Jesus! One of the guys on the force, a punk named Bernie made her last week and he wasn't the first one, he said.

—Oh, come on, Chris!

—Sure, it's the truth, Bernie said Dolores don't have no goddamn cunt, she has a fuckin' shoppin' bag in which she collects American cocks to take back across the border. Jesus, that kept some of the guys on edge the whole evening and what do you know, not a single one of the fartheads took his hands out of his pockets till they were safely home.

—Look, Chris, the traffic's just rolling by.

—Yeah, old father time don't stop for no one. Say, why don't we have a drink and maybe lunch around noon?

—I told you, Chris, I have Washington pumping hot air up my ass.

—Oh, sure, sure, he said.

—Look, I shouted suddenly, what's going on there with the guy in the yellow Camaro with the wide track oval tires and a spoiler on its rear?

—Yeah, Donnelly said, I been watching him, too.

—Search him, I shouted, strip his goddamn car!

—Okay, okay, take it easy, willya? Give me a minute.

Three minutes later Donnelly was back while I was striking another match to keep the heat on in the bowl.

—Okay, he said, the name's Meredith Sampson, six one, Cauc, born '43, father British physicist immigrated way back in '38, famous scientist, works at M.I.T. We checked that too, put a call through and got the answer in a second, yessir Doctor William G. Sampson is on the faculty. Young Meredith says he went across to write on the best cabrito restaurant for Vogue, that's legit too, I could smell the goddamn goat on his breath. He's on his way to San Antone to pick up a plane to New York City, we're letting him through, he's clean.

I took the pipe out of my mouth, knocked it against the heel of my boot as I began to walk away and put it in my pocket. I didn't want to waste time telling Donnelly what had suddenly occurred to me. I took the elevator down, repeating the name Meredith Sampson to myself again and again and knowing somewhere in my guts that he was connected with the ring but not being able to locate the information that was almost within my grasp. It hit me just when the elevator touched ground floor. Meredith Sampson. Me-redith. Sa-mpson. There it was. M.E.S.A.!

I walked across the hall, looking at the reception desk and saying, See you later, Dolores, whereupon she smiled broadly and said, Sure, honey, in that voice which foreigners and recent immigrants have which attempting what they believe to be American idiom invariably misplaces a crucial accent and screws up the phrase. I walked out into the street, went round the corner, and took some steps down to the basement garage, deliberately not going straight down to the basement in the elevator in order to be seen departing by Dolores. Jut as I was walking round the corner, I saw the yellow Camaro go up the street and switch on its turn signal to show Sampson was going to make a right turn, and for a moment I watched the light winking as if teasingly beckoning me to pursue while the spoiler that was stuck across the tail seemed like a barrier. But I wasn't going to see symbols in these things, and it was sufficient for the moment to notice that Sampson, by turning right, was heading for the interstate highway. I got into my red convertible Bug, and soon was on the highway myself.

The land was flat and dry, mostly uncultivated, and I could keep the Camaro in sight from a considerable distance. We were both doing eighty, when I noticed that Sampson began to go faster. We must have been driving steadily for some fifteen minutes when he began to go over eighty, and I figured that that was the time it took for him to get a message over the radio that he was being tailed. My suspicion about Dolores had been right. She hadn't been screwing freely with the cops for the shit of it; she relayed information to Harry Kateusz. It took her fifteen minutes to have the message relayed to Sampson because she wanted me to be under the impression that she had nothing to do with MESA.

Well, Sampson was pressing on it all right, he was way over a hundred. I decided to let him get out of sight for a few minutes, and then pressed right down on the gas myself. The Porsche engine of my VW cleared its throat and began the melody for which it was so assiduously tuned by Martin Martinelli, the mechanic in Upper Nyack who did all automotive jobs for me. I was doing a hundred in a second, a hundred and thirty in another ten and was up with the Camaro. I guess Sampson saw me over the horizon, probably did a double-take, figured out for himself that I had a hot Bug, and speeded up some more. I didn't expect his Camaro to go over a hundred and twenty, but Christ! He was doing a hundred and fifty-three by my speedometer when we were bumper to bumper. That was as fast as he could go, for I stuck to his bumper as if joined to it by a cabinet-maker's glue. He tried all kinds of tricks to get rid of me, braking suddenly to get me to crash into his rear, swerving to the left and to the right to get me to panic, taking corners so fast he came out of them sideways, and I must say I admired his driving. At one point he did a most daring thing. Some two hundred yards ahead of us was a bridge over a river. The road rose up slightly to make for the bridge, so that there was a kind of embankment on the side of the road that led to a fallow field, the slope being well graded but still being a drop of six to ten feet. The river was dry. Well, Sampson took all this information in, calculated his chances, all while driving at a hundred and fifty and now almost about to shoot over the bridge, and took what can appropriately be called the plunge. He swerved right, shot off the highway, his car leaped over the embankment, hit the ground where he steered it toward the river. I saw only his swerving and leaping over the embankment; for in that moment I, too, had taken in the information he had and interpreted his move, and so had flicked my wheel to the left and had shot off the embankment on the other side. That was of course what he'd hoped for. But what he didn't expect and was surprised to realize was that I held my car with the same precision and cool and made for the river-bed. Just when I was bumping over the stones and hearing the weeds scratching against the car-bottom, I looked to the right through the arch of the bridge and there was Sampson's Camaro similarly bumping over the river. I let him make the highway first, and in a moment was on his tail again. I caught his eye in his rear-view mirror and saw him grin and shake his head as if to say, We'd make a great team for the East African Safari, and I grinned back at him. He even relaxed the pace to a hundred and ten and we could have been a couple of stunt drivers coming back from some performance, cruising gently on our way home. We'd become kind of friendly, Sampson and me. He'd cruise along at a steady hundred, hundred and five, and then suddenly he'd try some new trick. At one point there was some highway construction going on and we had to leave the road and take a gravelled side-road before returning to the highway. Sampson took the chance to zig-zag across the gravel, thereby hoping that flying stones from his rear tires would hit my windshield. Well, they hit the windshield all right, like a bunch of hailstones, but Martin Martinelli had prepared the car to meet a worse contingency by replacing the windshield with bulletproof glass.

Well, in this considerably diverting manner, we made San Antone and parked side by side at the airport. We shook hands and Sampson said, Well, I guess we made the flight, and looking at his watch, added, Two minutes to return the key to the car rental agency, five to check in, and we'll be in the plane.

—What about the security check, Sampson? I asked.

—Sure, the security check, he said, but there's nothing on me that the electronic device will pick up unless my balls have turned to brass.

We laughed together as we walked quickly to the terminal building. He returned the key to the rental firm and I walked with him to the Braniff check-in counter where he produced his ticket for the clerk, and while the latter was checking it, I said, Okay, Sampson, it's been good travelling with you, see you some time. Maybe we could do the Monte Carlo Rally, we'd make a great team.

—Sure thing, he said, collecting his boarding pass and walking away.

When the plane had taken off, I called Dallas, Washington and New York and told them that Sampson was on the flight and they should tail him wherever he got off. While my general instinct to follow Sampson had been correct, I believed now that he was not Mesa. I went back to my car, deciding to wait, for I believed the Camaro would soon be picked up and lead me to Mesa. There was one fact that had prompted me to let Sampson go and stick to the Camaro: when he had returned the car-key, he had produced no papers, settled no account, but simply smiled at the girl who said, We'll bill Vogue.

Even as I was walking back to my car, I saw a heavy middle-aged man putting a rather large suitcase in the Camaro's trunk. He wore green corduroy trousers and a blue sport coat; a felt hat, black-rimmed spectacles, and carried a raincoat on his arm. He entered the car rather laboriously, throwing the raincoat in, took some time studying the dials on the dashboard, switched on the motor and slowly drove away as if he were driving the family Impala to church. I tailed him somewhat half-heartedly trying not to think that I might have made a mistake chasing Sampson in the first place. The man drove so slowly and carefully you'd have thought there were children playing all over the highway. I was beginning to get depressed when I realized that he'd taken the highway south, to the border. I knew now that the Sampson drive to San Antone had been a clever diversionary trick and that the car had never been intended to go ten miles past the border checkpoint. Well, I had plenty of time to reflect, fill up gas, stop to get a hamburger, make a call to New York, pull up into a rest area and snooze for twenty minutes, and to continue tailing the Camaro which proceeded at fifty miles an hour.

I could see the tower of the El Dorado motel and could not help thinking of myself standing on the roof there looking across the border earlier the same day when the man in the Camaro turned into a street and entered the driveway of a house. The garage door was closed, so he parked just in front of the door. In spite of the Camaro's wide-opening door, it cost him considerable labor to get out of the car. He began to walk across the lawn in the direction of the entrance to the house. An Alsatian dog came running up to him when he was in the middle of the lawn, and he greeted the dog with, Hi, there, Toppsy, how've you been, boy, what've you been doing, son, while papa's been travellin', heh, Toppsy? The dog returned the greeting by rising up on his hindlegs so that he could place his paws on his master's shoulders and lick his face. You missed me, didya, Toppsy? Boy, did I miss you too!

Impressed by this statement, the dog pushed the man back so that he fell upon the grass; and the next moment the two of them were rolling about the lawn, the man carrying on a declaration of profound love for the dog and the dog continuing to lick his face and neck. I was almost convinced that I had made a mistake and was about to drive away and was wondering whether I should save the day by taking Dolores out and maybe drop an egg or two in her shopping bag to test Donnelly's notion of her when I suddenly saw another connection: Toppsy! Toppsy. Top. Table-top. Table. Mesa. The sequence was inescapable.

Just then a young man came out of the house, said, Hi, dad, had a good trip?, received no answer for the man was still busy playing with the dog, went to the garage, opened the door, drove the car in and closed the garage door from the inside. I waited. Twenty minutes went by, but the young man remained inside. So, I'd been right, the car was hot, and he was working on it. What I needed to do was to interrupt him. The other man and the dog had gone into the house by now, and so I walked up to the front door and rang the bell. To my astonishment, it was the young man who opened the door.

—Pardon me, I said, I left my car outside your house and on returning found the battery had gone dead; do you think you could bring your car out so that I could run a jump-cable to the battery and start it?

—Sure, he said.

—Thanks, I said, I greatly appreciate it.

He walked across the lawn, opened the garage door and soon had the Camaro parked next to my car out on the roadside. In the meanwhile I had returned to my car and had called the force to send in all available units. A minute after the Camaro was next to my Bug, five police cars came screaming down and as soon as the officers emerged from the cars I shouted at them, Search that goddamn Camaro!

—Hey, what's this? the young man asked, and a cop said to him, Put your balls into your mouth, mister.

—What the hell is all this? the young man demanded.

—O fuck this punk, the cop said and knocked him unconscious with one blow across the jaw.

The older man emerged from the house, the Alsatian with him, and said, What's going on? The dog seemed bewildered for a moment and then began to bark.

—Oh, shut up! a cop said to the dog, but the dog only barked the more.

—What are you doing to my rented car? the man asked.

The dog gave a howl.

—Screw you, said the cop to the dog.

—Can someone please explain? the man said somewhat helplessly.

—You're the one who'll have to explain, Mr. Charrington, the cop said to him. Take him in, Norm.

Another cop came up to Charrington and told him to go with him to one of the police-cars. He was driven away, the wheelspin from the car making a screaming sound and leaving black rubber-marks on the road. Seeing his master go, the dog began to bark even more loudly.

—O fuck this son of a bitch, the cop said, taking out his gun and shooting the dog through the head.

The men who had been searching the Camaro came up with nothing.

—Take it to the shop and strip it, I said.

Ten minutes later, I was in the shop, too, at the back of the police station, watching while the men stripped the car. They found nothing. Ah, shit, I thought, there's going to be a whole fuck to pay for this.

They were grilling Charrington in the office. His story was that he'd flown in from Chicago where he'd gone to make a deal with a meat-packing firm. Charrington, Charrington, I thought, there was something peculiar about the name. He said he'd wanted to rent a Vega at San Antone but they only had this Camaro. Then it occurred to me. Charrington! Why, it was obvious. Charrington,

Chair. Chair, Table. Table, Mesa. It also occurred to me that maybe Mesa was not a person, but that it was a code name for the entire operation.

—Okay, Charrington, the officer said to him, I don't have to inform you that the F.B.I, is going in for pickled balls in a big way this year, so let's see if you can do better.

Another officer was going through the contents of Charrington's pockets that had been emptied out on a table. There was the usual trash, and the only interesting item was a piece of paper with four phone numbers scribbled on it. I took that and went to a private office and called the numbers. The first was answered by a girl in a sweet voice who said, We love you for calling The Timid Man's Massage Parlor, will you give me the pleasure of touching you? The second one answered with, All Braniff lines are temporarily busy . . . . The third simply said, The Spoils. I took that to be a restaurant and said, Say, what's on the menu today? There was a silence at the other end, and I said, I was thinking of reserving a table. The phone was abruptly put down, and in that moment the answer came to me.

I ran back to the body shop, and even as I was entering it, I shouted, Tear that damned spoiler apart!

That's where we found it, the spoiler was packed with two million dollars' worth of the stuff. I'd been staring at the fucking thing all the way to San Antone and back.

That evening I took Dolores out to dinner at the town's only Chinese restaurant where she ordered two vodkas to commence with and then studying the menu with the bold sketch of a pig-tailed profile upon it, told the waiter to bring her a charcoal broiled steak and French fries.

—I'm not going to eat no commie food, she said to me. So, she added, you got the stuff.

—Sure, I said, we got the stuff, but we don't have to talk about my work.

—Okay, honey, she said, you sit tight on your fanny and I'll just wiggle my boobs at you and we'll have a swell time.

—Oh, come on, Dolores, I've had a tough day.

—What did Donnelly tell you about me?

—Who's Donnelly?

—Aw, shit, what's this, an evening out or goddamn visit to the morgue? You going to sit there like a bloodless corpse and give me the shit about who's Donnelly?

—I'm sorry, Dolores, I thought maybe you'd want to listen to soft music and have a good meal.

—Music! Jesus, listen to that! A couple of Arabs on bagpipes could do better than that crap. Let me tell you, Walt, I majored in music and played the solo in Stravinsky's Capriccio for Piano and Orchestra for my masters. No, don't say it!

—What?

—You were just going to say you hit the wrong chord, weren't you? Jesus, you guys think yourselves so witty!

The food arrived and there was a moment's silence while the waiter served it. I was beginning to wonder how I was going to go through another hour with Dolores when, the waiter departing, she said, cutting her steak: Go ahead, enjoy your lobster balls, they probably come canned from Hong Kong and are more likely to be raw canine balls than anything made of lobster meat, go ahead, have a great time. It's the East's revenge for having suffered western imperialism for so long. They don't have the technology, so they're going to get us with heroin, Japanese cars and dogs' balls.

—Pardon me, Dolores, but where did you pick up all this bullshit?

—Not from your ass, mister.

—Well, this is just great. I take a dame out to dinner, and to anyone watching us in this dim light I must appear a lucky guy with a stunning dame next to me, white pearls at her neck, her low-cut pink dress spilling out nine-tenths of her tits that've got even the air conditioning on heat, but what am I getting here, heap upon heap of bullshit!

—Why, Walt, there's no need to spoil this dinner with foul talk. Let me give you something.

She inserted two fingers in the cleavage of her breasts, plucked out a ball of cottonwool and put it to my nose, saying, Take it, honey, it's the sweetest smell you ever had, I dabbed it with a French perfume. Keep it in your pocket for when you're lonely, you can breathe in the real thing now.

The little gesture had a potent effect upon me, making me momentarily dizzy and then not a little lustful.

—This wine's okay, too, she said. You have a great taste for the good things in life, it's a pleasure to be dated by a sophisticated guy.

She drank some wine, laughing softly, showing her small white teeth.

—Do you know the difference, she asked, picking up the cork and reading the impression upon it, between Mise en bouteille au château and Mise au domaine?

—Well, it's . . .

—No, it's not what you think, she said, laughing. Let me show you. This, she said, putting the cork very softly to her mouth, holding it delicately between her teeth and touching it with her tongue, is Mise en bouteille au château, and this—she took the cork away and put her hand below the table-cloth where I could not entirely see but it was apparent that she'd raised her skirt—is Mise au domaine. She brought the cork up and put it quickly against my nose just as she had done with the ball of cottonwool, saying, See?

—Christ, Dolores, you're crazy! I said, finding the wine-soaked cork exude a far stronger bouquet.

—Just thought you'd like to know the possibilities, she said. No one eats lobster balls who doesn't unconsciously want his own balls eaten. I know your secret lusts, Walt, you don't have to play the quiet gentleman with me and hope for a satisfactory seduction, and nor am I a goddamn whore.

—Oh, come on, Dolores, I thought you were beginning to have a good time.

—Sure, I'm having a great time. Wasn't that what that prickless pig Donnelly said to you? What a smell! he said, wasn't that it? Well, you give him that cork and ask him to lick it off. He'll do it, too, the pervert. Jesus, do you think I'm just a dumb receptionist? You guys think the minorities are there just to be screwed.

—Who said anything about the minorities, for god's sake? And besides you went to Vassar.

59

—Who said anything about Vassar? Don't try cheap irony on me.

She was about to say more but stopped suddenly. I looked in the direction at which she had begun to stare and saw a young man in a white double-breasted suit with a fawn-colored wide-brimmed felt hat tilted over his head slowly walking across the restaurant. The hat was pulled well over his eyes and the dim light also made it difficult to identify him. In any case, not expecting anyone I knew to come to the restaurant, it did not occur to me that I should search my memory for recognition, and so merely took him for someone Dolores probably knew. He walked up to the bar in the far corner of the room, ordered a drink, knocked it back in a second and turned around. Dolores had continued to watch him and had stopped eating. She was sitting upright, her hands in her lap under the table-cloth. The man took a step in our direction, his hands in his pockets. I saw Dolores's hand come up with a jerk from under the table, holding a gun. In the same moment I was aware that the man had pulled his right hand out of his pocket, and all of a sudden there was a burst of gunfire. Dolores's shot missed the man and hit the Chinese barman between the eyes, sending his brain splashing against the liquor bottles behind him. The man's shot hit Dolores in the neck, and her head slumped against her half-eaten steak.

The man walked right out and was over the border in two minutes. Just as he was walking steadily away, gun in hand, ready to shoot anyone who stirred, I caught his eyes. It was Meredith Sampson who'd never caught the plane east but had flown right back, having neatly got me off his ass in San Antone. I figured it out in an instant. The lady slumped beside me, her blood overflowing from the plate that she had recently eaten from, had been Mesa. I checked her purse later and found a card in it on which was printed:

Mexican Emancipation, S.A.
M E S A

60

The same card had been found at several assassinations in Mexico City, Guadalajara, San Francisco and Atlantic City, and in each case the clues led to political and criminal figures.

Jerry Biderman called me from L.A. that night and congratulated me for cracking the Mesa mystery. We talked for some twenty minutes mainly about the game between the Dallas Cowboys and the Miami Dolphins and just before hanging up, Jerry said, Say hello to Hulme for me.

—To whom?

—Hulme. You've seen him around, haven't you? Pink roast-beef cheeks, droopy moustache.

—Sure, I've seen him around. I didn't know he was here.

—He's there.

—What's he doing here?

—Observing.

The next morning I slept late and when I went down to the hotel desk just before noon, found the following handwritten message: Didn't wish to wake you and have to dash up north. No doubt there'll be another opportunity, for in spite of everything one can't escape space and time. Hastily then: just wanted to say your method is sound, the results impressive. Things could follow, of course, especially when there's lightning and then thunder and there's the wretched business of the waves on the shore. *Which shore* hardly matters. Some puzzles remain puzzles, nevertheless, and all the computerised scrutiny of the forensic lab just doesn't help. So much for facts! One is obliged sometimes to close an unsolved case when the facts we've pieced together fit the picture perfectly and yet don't get us anywhere. Though we do continue to speculate and produce a new theory every ten or twenty years. As in the case of Jack the Ripper. We can keep on speculating and be intellectually intoxicated by the conviction that we're near the truth. And we might well persuade an entire generation that our version is in fact closest to the truth. When another clue is discovered. Or another mind comes along and insists it's all a matter of re-investigation and re-interpretation. It does pass the time awfully pleasantly, don't you think? Have you, when looking for finger-prints on a window-sill, ever had the startling

61

experience of suddenly seeing your own reflection in the window-pane?

There, with that absurdly irrelevant question, the message ended; there was no signature appended to it, only the capital letter H. I crumpled the paper into a ball and threw it into a waste can beside the receptionist's desk, saying, So what else is new?

The girl behind the desk, mistakenly thinking that I'd spoken to her, said, I'm sorry, I don't understand.

V

Marriage and Settlement

When I returned to the house, Rosemary was sitting on the steps of the back porch, a young man with short cut dark hair next to her holding her hand in both of his and looking at her with what one was supposed to understand was 100% love.

—Oh, hello, Walt, Rosemary said, a bit early in the morning for you to be about, isn't it? I know, don't tell me, you haven't slept all night. That's okay, I understand, I saw you running after a straw-haired girl, and, well, as I say, I understand. Warm night, good hay in the barn, and everything. Hey, this is Jay Rosenquist. Jay, this is Walt I told you about.

—Hi, Walt, said Jay, looking deeply into Rosemary's eyes. There seemed to be a permanent smile upon his face and when he uttered a few words as now he hardly opened his mouth, only widened his smile into a grin and let the words escape through his teeth.

—Pleased to meet you, Jay.

—The feeling's mutual, he said through his perma-press mouth, his eyes still upon Rosemary.

—That was no straw-haired girl, I said to Rosemary, I was running after Fingers Dawson.

—But it wasn't Fingers Dawson, Rosemary said.

—The point is I thought he was, I said. You saw us fire, didn't you?

—No, I was dancing with Jay.

—Sure, honey, we really had a great dance, said Jay.

—Oh, come on, Walt, you don't have to make excuses to me. Sure, she was dressed like a cowboy, many girls dress like that in the country, and there's nothing perverse about chasing a girl who looks like a boy, no one's going to spread malicious rumors about you.

—But it was a man, I tell you. Only, it wasn't Fingers Dawson.

—Anyone could have told you it wasn't Fingers, for it was Mary Lou Lawson. She'll do anything to get out of a dance.

—It was a great dance, said Jay, getting a little closer to Rosemary and rubbing his polyester nose against her hair.

—Even dress up like a man, Rosemary went on. You want to be careful, Walt, Mary Lou Lawson has the devil in her. Mess with her—you might as well say your prayers and prepare to meet your maker, she's like sinking sand, she'll suck you right down to hell.

—Ah, sand, moonlight, the lapping waves, said Jay. Honey, why don't we go to the Caribbean for our honeymoon?

—Honeymoon? I said.

—Sure, said Rosemary. You've been wanting to know all about Mary Lou Lawson, you haven't given me a chance to say that Jay and I are going to be married.

—Congratulations, I said.

—Grenada, Martinique, Guadeloupe, what do you say, honey? said the duralon hero.

—Sure, honey, Rosemary said, and turning to me, added, What's more Fingers Dawson called last night.

—Why should he do that?

—Just to show you how smart he is, I guess.

—What did he say?

—Nothing. Just sang a verse of some crazy ballad. I memorised it for you:

> Tell Walt that the shadows in the barn
> Are those of Mary Lou Lawson
> And not as he mistakenly imagines
> Of the fugitive Fingers Dawson.

—Uh-huh, I don't believe that, I said. Fingers wouldn't use proper names for a rhyme. It's cheap.

—Well, thanks a lot! Next time I hear a verse on the phone I'll know better than to take the trouble memorising it.

—I'm not blaming you, Rosemary, I said. I had a tough night.

—We've had a beautiful night, said Jay Rosenquist whom I believed by now to be an idiot.

—Well, please yourself, Rosemary said. Jay and I are to be married next week, and you are supposed to give me away.

Rosemary told me afterwards when we were alone together that Jay was only twenty years old and that they had spent the night lying in a field where the wheat had just been harvested. We just lay there, she said, looking up at the stars, just holding hands. Finally, I kissed him, just a gentle little peck. He drew back at once as if in astonishment, or disbelief that the wonderful thing called sex was happening to him; his mind appeared to be clouded over for a couple of minutes, then it suddenly cleared, for he smiled and said, Rosemary will you marry me? Oh, what a sweet thought! I cried embracing him and in the process driving him on his back so that I pressed upon him. He received me kind of passively, letting me drive my hands into his shirt, feeling his smooth chest, like I thought a Victorian maiden must have surrendered herself to a middle-aged satyr. I guess I was quite brutal for a few minutes, but I couldn't help it, tearing at his shirt and kissing his hairless chest and everything, getting my hands down his jeans and into them, too.

—Oh, for god's sake, Rosemary!

—Sure, why not? And what do you know, Walt, I couldn't find his cock.

—Maybe he leaves it at home in a silk purse.

—Maybe, Rosemary said. But I agreed, saying, Sure, honey, I'll marry you. He was so thrilled, he got up and did a little dance. His family has oil in Oklahoma.

—Oh ho!

—And why not?

—Ho, ho, ho!

—Oh, come on, Walt, what's a girl supposed to do, wait for the stock market to improve?

—Do you, Oil-well, take this ruthless, avaricious woman for your wife? Gurgle, gurgle, gurgle, Ho, ho, what a marriage! Gush, gush, gush.

—It's the only way I can see things turning for the better in

America. And besides, Jay needs someone strong to look after him, he's such a weak little darling.

—Gush, gush.

Poker called from inside the house. She was in the kitchen baking a pecan pie, her sleeves rolled up and her hair combed back and brought together in a rubber band.

—Oh, hi, maw, I said, what is it?

—Well, you could at least have washed your face before coming to see me, she said. You look as though you've been lying in some field with your face pressed to the dirt. There's a guy come to see you, he's in the den. What've you been doing all night, screwing cows?

—I was just chopping some lumber, Poker.

—What, you fixing to build that shed you've been talking about?

—Who's this guy?

—Sounds foreign to me, Poker said. Very ruddy complexion, purple blotches on the cheeks, fat, said his name was Hamm.

—Hamm?

—It could've been Holmes, or maybe Hammond. Depends on how clearly he spoke in that moment, what trouble he took to pronounce all the syllables. Trouble is I was shelling pecans at the time and happened to crack a nut just when he spoke his name. It could be his name is Crick and he said, My name is Crick, and then when the coincidence of his saying his name and my cracking the nut had passed, he added, Hm, or made some sound in his throat and I thought that was his name, Hm, and when I told him to go wait in the den and had collected the pecans together for the pie, the Hm had become enlarged in my mind to Hamm. Maybe he's English. The English are like that. A guy gave me his card once and it said on it Beauchamp of Leicester, and just when I was looking at it, he said Beacha Molesstah, and I thought he was telling me, while I perused his name on the card, that he was some cop looking for a beach molester, and thought maybe he was an Italian.

—I knew a girl in Mississippi whose parents, Mr. and Mrs. Matthew Stone, had given her the name Cherry, and all her

66

friends called her Pippa.

—Why, I knew Cherry Stone! She introduced breast-sag at the campuses, always wore green, began to be called Avocado, and ended up by being known as Ava.

—That's Pippa all right! Say, I said, pointing to the pot, is that coffee hot?

—Yeah, and there's some fresh cream in the ice-box, Poker said. You can have a couple of oatmeal cookies, too, if you like, I made 'em an hour ago.

—That'll be just fine, I said, but I think I'll make myself a ham sandwich first.

—Let me make it for you, Poker said. You want some mustard on it?

—Sure.

—I'll cut you a pickled gherkin and a tomato to go with it.

—Don't cut that ham too thin, Poker!

—I've packed your bags already for the flight to Miami. They've hired two jumbo jets to take everyone there. For the wedding.

By the time I went to the den, my visitor had left. I found a note by the fire place which read: E.g., Disneyworld. The fantastic as living theatre. Comic-book figures larger than life. Every image a representation of unreality. Pilgrims come there by the million. Not a single incredulous soul among them. The question then is not one of belief. What then? H.

I threw the note away at the airport when I joined Rosemary's 747 for her wedding. We were entertained by two movies during the flight, 'The Bride Wore Black' and 'For Whom the Bell Tolls.' It was apparent that the person who had been told to pick two suitable movies for a wedding party on its flight across America had quickly looked through some catalogue and chosen what sounded appropriate for the occasion. The first movie turned out to be in French without any subtitles and was about some crazy dame killing a whole bunch of hoodlums in a series of fantastic accidents, and the second was obviously a rare copy of an original American film, for it had been dubbed into Spanish. One woman on my flight began to sob and said, How can Jennifer Jones do that to me, talk like she was some Chicana?

The two planes, his and hers, flew side by side right across the blue-skied land. The flight plan entailed a great circle over America, so that rising out of the middle-west we flew over the Rio Grande, across the deserts of Arizona and southern California, up to the forests of Oregon and Washington, swooped down over Old Faithful in Wyoming, coasted across the line dividing the Dakotas, skimmed over the great lakes, descending down to make a loop over Niagara Falls, rose over the stacked-up traffic circling above New York, came down upon the nation's capital and rose again for the final southward thrust to Miami. Deplaning in the Florida sunshine, one guest was heard to say, How come we missed the Grand Canyon?

The wedding took place on a ranch operated by Promise of Motherhood, Inc., an organization that marketed happy marriages throughout the country. We drove up to a vast parking lot at the entrance to the ranch and abandoned our cars there for ornate horse-drawn carriages, broughams and landaus that had been painstakingly copied from the best European models of the eighteenth and nineteenth centuries, the one reserved for the bride being modelled after the coach in which Queen Elizabeth II rode to her coronation. The procession of carriages entered the gates of what appeared to be a huge estate, a dozen Cuban refugees dressed up like British Beefeaters guarding the entrance. The land had been landscaped to resemble farms in France and in the distance one could see French-looking shepherds and milkmaids going about their business. A couple of windmills imported from Holland stood upon two hilltops. The main building, in which the wedding ceremony took place, was built to look like a castle on the Rhine.

I entered the Hall of Betrothal with Rosemary at my arm walking through two lines of liveried trumpeters. Inside, we were led to the center of a vast circular room with a continuous wall on which were projected in an ever moving succession photographs of the altars of the great cathedrals of the world, and since Rosemary had indicated on the form she had had to fill up for Promise of Motherhood, Inc., that she belonged to no church and considered herself fortunate to have no beliefs whatsoever, the pictures of the altars alternated with shots of temples in Benares, mosques in Istanbul and Cairo, various religious buildings in Jerusalem, the Pope blessing the crowds in the Vatican, cripples arriving in Lourdes on charter flights from Canada, pilgrims slaughtering sheep, goats and camels in Mecca, the Mayan pyramids in the Yucatan, the Archbishop of Canterbury walking in his garden and leaning toward a rose-bush to inhale the perfume of a rose, Hindus apparently praying but quite obviously urinating in the Ganges, a crowd of Italians carrying the Virgin through the streets of Naples, and Archbishop Makarios of Cyprus alighting from a helicopter. I heard a guest say to another, The world's rich in symbols, and receive the reply, Harry, you're always seeing weird meanings in things.

When the guests had all been shown to their places, the succession of photographs was switched off and movie clips began to be projected on the wall, beginning with Elizabeth Taylor sailing up the Nile to meet Mark Antony. At the same time a female choir began to hum melodiously on the quadrophonic sound system upon whose angelic hymning voices was superimposed a succession of fragments from Frank Sinatra, Dean Martin, Sammy Davis, Jr., Doris Day, more Frank Sinatra and a lot more Doris Day.

The hall darkened, the mixed media show faded away with What will be, will be. A spotlight came on, threw its beam to the ceiling and revealed a bald man with grey eyebrows and whiskers suspended below the ceiling, dressed in a costume which was priestly without signifying a particular religion or sect. Just as the spotlight illuminated his benign, smiling face, the ceiling lit up to show a blue sky with little puffs of white clouds. A voice came on: Lo, the Lord of Weddings descendeth. At that moment the Lord began to come down, floating easily and effortlessly, an effect contrived with the greatest cunning for no mechanical devices or stage effects could be observed. By now Jay Rosenquist and Rosemary stood side by side at the front of the assembled guests before a table covered with a purple cloth. The Lord of Weddings descended and stood exactly opposite the couple, two feet away, the table behind him. No wires, ropes or chains appeared to be attached to him.

The blue sky vanished and a subdued lighting now illuminated the hall. In the meanwhile, the circular wall had disappeared and the hall had become rectangular with gothic arches vaulting across the room. The Lord of Weddings gestured with his hand to indicate to the bride and bridegroom to come forward to the table where he placed a form before them. They were given a golden pen and asked to make check-marks in the appropriate boxes next to the various questions. Rosemary had only one box to check, indicating that she was voluntarily taking Jay Rosenquist for her husband. Jay, however, had a long list to go through in which he had to check boxes which signified his affirmation to guarantee a number of rights to Rosemary in the event of the marriage ending in a divorce. The Lord of Weddings took the form, folded it and put it away in a pocket in his gown which looked like a kaftan made of scarlet velvet. He produced another piece of paper which he gave Jay to study later. It was an invitation from a subsidiary of Promise of Motherhood, Inc., calling itself Marruj DizZolvers, Inc., and offered a discount rate for a divorce at any future date provided Jay and Rosemary filled in a coupon and mailed it within thirty days of their wedding. The offer was made in a humorous language with numerous misspellings and was bordered by comical cartoons which revealed a lasting marriage to be boring, painful, built upon lies and deceptions, against human instinct, redundant in the modern age, and bad for the American economy.

The lights went out for a second during which the Lord of Weddings disappeared through a trap-door in the floor. Jay and Rosemary turned around and took their first steps together as man and wife. Their steps pressed upon some rubber pads beneath the carpet and that set in motion a mechanism which produced a shower of rose-petals which continued to fall as they walked toward the table at the rear of the hall where a banquet had been laid out.

The guests arose and began to congratulate one another at the beautiful simplicity of the ceremony but were soon attracted to the tables of food and champagne that had appeared along the circular wall. The couple was taken away to Immortality

Corner where the event of their matrimony was inscribed upon a golden plaque upon which they etched their signatures and had the satisfaction of seeing the plaque fixed upon a marble wall, a Polaroid photograph of it taken and presented to the bride. They were then invited to choose a setting for their wedding photograph. Promise of Motherhood, Inc., had constructed replicas of the steps of St. Paul's cathedral, London, the Sacré Coeur, Paris, and several other famous places of worship, and if the couple chose one which did not exist in replica then a slide of it would be projected against the wall; they were assured that the photograph would look as real as the replicas. Rosemary decided that she did not want a religious background and asked them to create a montage of the Niagara Falls superimposed upon the Grand Canyon, which they did in two seconds.

A helicopter took the couple away to Miami airport from where they flew to an island in the Caribbean. I wrote out a check for fifty-five thousand dollars to Promise of Motherhood, Inc., and then rented a car to drive back to New York, having business on the way in Atlanta, Greensboro and Washington, D.C. When a week later, I entered my apartment, the phone was ringing.

—Hi, Walt, Rosemary's voice came over so clearly she could have been in her apartment on 17th Street.

—Hi, Rosemary, I said, where are you? In St. Croix? Montego Bay? Port of Spain?

—Shit, no, she said, I'm in my apartment on 17th. Why don't you come on over, Walt?

A man entered the elevator when I got out of it on Rosemary's floor. I thought I recognized him and almost said Hello and turned to look but the door had closed upon the portly form and the elevator had begun to descend.

Rosemary opened the door quickly and turned away, not even greeting me, saying: Of course, I cannot prevent people from thinking that I married Jay Rosenquist for his money, but the truth is I loved the guy, he was so devoted to me, I could have leaned back against a pillow, an arm behind my head and one of my breasts falling out of a pale yellow silk gown, and he would have suckled there like a baby all night, he was that devoted.

I had not realized when she had called me that she would have company, for now, having admitted me to the apartment, she had turned around to continue what was obviously a statement she had begun before she opened the door for me. Talking, she walked into the sitting room, dropped into a sofa like someone who is exhausted, and said, What do you think, Walt?

There was no one else in the room and I said, Rosemary, to whom were you talking just now?

—Oh, I was just rehearsing, she said. Pru Essenfoot has gone and called Helen Kreutzer for an item in Helen's gossip column and Helen's sending Mildred Belinoski to interview me, so I've been rehearsing my statement. It could lead to an appearance on a talk show, Helen said. Maybe I should leave out the bit about my tit, but maybe not. This is New York. Everyone's after a thrill.

—Rosemary, who was that guy who just took the elevator down? He could only have been coming from here.

—That was a detective I hired, she said.

—He looked familiar, I said.

—Yeah, she said, he looks like a picture of G. K. Chesterton. His name's Hume.

—Not Hulme?

—Could be. Or maybe Home. But he said Hume.

—What do you want a detective for, Rosemary?

—Look at all this junk, she said, pointing to a pile of papers on a table beside her. My divorce settlement, for god's sake! Three oil-wells in Oklahoma. Ten thousand acres in west Texas. A house in Key West. I feel sorry for Jay.

—Why is that?

—Wouldn't you feel sorry for someone who loved you so much? Jesus, I'm exhausted!

—What went wrong, Rosemary?

—See this? she said, holding the little finger of her right hand in the palm of her left hand, bringing the thumb and fingers together to clasp the little finger in such a way that only the tip of the little finger showed. That's how big his cock was, she said. What's a girl supposed to do, one has longings, and what good is a soggy little asparagus tip?

72

—Oh, that's too bad, I said.

—It's downright tragic, she said. I had to have a showdown with old Marvin Rosenquist, Jay's stingy old father. He's the one with the properties.

—But what's Hulme supposed to do?

—Hume?

—Yeah.

—He's going west to check into these properties. But, Walt, I need you. I have a suspicion that Hume's not a detective at all. I was thinking of following him west, but I don't think I could go alone.

—And you want me to go with you?

—I was hoping you'd offer to go.

—Then why did you hire Hulme?

—I'm miserably rich, Walt. What I pay Hume comes right off my taxes. Besides, he's kind of quaint. I'm interested in him. He is not without curiosity. It'll be intriguing to see what he observes.

—But what exactly do you expect a detective to find?

—What it is.

—What's that?

—What he finds.

—Oh!

—Will you go, Walt?

—And what should I do if I go?

—See what Hume's up to.

—Hulme?

—Yeah.

—But what do you think might be happening out west?

—Look, Walt, I have ten thousand goddamn acres in west Texas. I want to know what the hell they look like.

—It's desert, surely. I was out there in '49 when Lizard-eyes Harry was wanted for murder in San Angelo. I tracked him down south of Midland and east of El Paso. It was a desert out there, just a fine light brown dust with maybe a table-top somewhere on the horizon. For three days there were just the two of us on the land. Lizard-eyes out on the horizon on the west and me on the eastern rim of the desert. We might as well have stood still where we were, it made no difference, for he was always stuck out to the west and I miles behind him on the east. It was like when you're in a plane and there's another plane in the distance going the same direction and you're both doing six hundred miles an hour and yet appear to be stuck there at thirty-thousand feet, getting nowhere. Finally, Lizard-eyes turned around and began to ride in my direction, and we met. You could've rode faster and caught up with me, why didn't ya? he demanded. I didn't want to panic your horse, I said. Well, hi, Walt, he said, it's good to meet ya at last. Hi, Lizard, I said, it's been a good ride. Sure, he said, there's nuthin' like ridin' west, not even my maw's pancakes gave me the same satisfaction as waitin' for the goddamn sun to come up from behind me and drop out there in the west. Why don't we ride across the border, I suggested, and drink some decent beer? It's thirsty work watching the sun come up and go down, day after day. Sure is, Lizard-eyes said, gives a man a mighty thirst, and this is the big country. There's not much for the sun to do here, he added, but watch a man tryin' more and more desperately to creep under his own shadow. Well, let's go get us some decent beer, I said.

—But that's not true, Rosemary said, you didn't go across the border to drink beer.

—You're damn right we didn't, I said. He was a murderer, wasn't he? And I had to take him in. We just kept riding and talking. He liked to think he was heading south when it was quite clear that we were aiming for San Angelo.

—Why should he have given himself up so meekly? Rosemary asked.

—Did he have a choice? He couldn't have continued to ride west, for I'd have stuck to him like a mussel to a rock. It was better for him to have me as a companion, someone to tell stories to. And sure, he knew when I said south I meant north. He knew too they had a rope waiting for him in San Angelo, that there would be five thousand people to watch him hang from it. Better, he figured, to die among witnesses than to come to nothing in the desert. There are not even buzzards out there in the desert to watch you die, so what's the use of that kind of heroism? But in the crowd maybe there'd be a woman with tears in her eyes.

74

—Sure, I was sorry for the guy when I saw him hang, Rosemary said, I cried like he was my own brother.

—What can Hulme do out there?

—He's interested, Rosemary said. He was very anxious to take on the job. There's the house in Key West, I told him, the oil-wells in Oklahoma and the land out in west Texas, where do you want to go first? He seemed already to have made up his mind to go to Texas. I told him, Look, there's not even a Holiday Inn for two hundred miles, but he said, Sure, lady, I know. There are some madmen in this world, Walt. Full of their own crazy ideas.

—How did you find him?

—Whom?

—Yeah, Hulme.

—He gave a lecture to my alma mater on investigative procedures which I missed. So I called him and said I was sorry I'd missed his lecture and we began to talk about various things. Oh, this and that. About some paintings Jay bought me for my wedding present and how to have them copied so that the originals could be put in a bank vault. He had been following the trail of some smugglers of Mayan sculpture from the Yucatan and described the difficulties of trying to tell the originals from the fakes. Oh, we had a long chat. And then I said, Hey, would you like to investigate something for me? And he said, Sure, lady. But, Walt, let me tell you my great secret! See these paintings?

I glanced quickly at the walls and pointing to the pictures one by one, said: Stella, Francis, Louis, Francis, Francis, Stella, Newman, Stella. Sure, I see them.

—Well, I called Helen Kreutzer and told her I had a nice little para for her gossip column about how I got the pictures copied and had the originals hidden away in a bank, and she said, Why, Rosemary, that's a great story, I'll get Mildred Belinoski to write it up, and there it was in Helen's column the next day, Pru Essenfoot brought me the paper to show me the piece. As a result, everyone who comes here says, Fantastic! These copies could have fooled me, they say, they're just fantastic. What do you know, Walt, they're not copies at all but the originals. By making everyone believe they're copies I have the best insurance and save myself thirty-three thousand dollars a year in insurance premiums. Isn't that just madly clever of me? So, will you go west with me?

—Sure, we could go west, I said. I have some things to finish in the east first though.

—I wish I knew what the land's like out there, she said.

—Pretty empty, I said. There's a highway that goes right through it, though. People drive past at ninety miles an hour, windows up, air conditioning on high, the radio playing a cool music, only the driver awake, just about. They're all making for the motels in El Paso. A swim in the pool and color TV after the steak and French fries is what they have on their minds, and the next day's drive across Arizona.

—I wonder what Hume will think of it, Rosemary said.

—He must have an idea, I said, why else should he want to head for the desert first? He must know something.

—Well, when will you be through with your business in the east?

—Oh, I don't know, I said. I've to fly to Washington tomorrow for a conference with Jerry Biderman. I'll have some idea then.

The door swung open and Betty Long looked in its direction anxiously from behind the counter just next to the coffee urn, for Betty daydreamed daily that a smart young businessman driving from San Francisco to New York would stop outside for gas and come in for coffee and, seeing Betty, fall in love with her and immediately persuade her tyrannical father to let her marry him and take her away to the big city where Betty could buy the dresses she'd seen advertised in the New Yorker by Saks of Fifth Avenue and take the poodle out for a walk in Central Park. For a hundred miles on either side along the highway from the diner, where she worked as a waitress, and the gasoline station outside, there was nothing. The wind blew every night, throwing up the sand against the windows. Her brother George, working the pumps outside either in blowing sand or snow, in hundred plus heat or subzero cold, hated her for having the better job in the family, and once when a neatly dressed man driving a Buick Riviera had said she had pretty blue eyes, George, who had followed him into the diner, immediately threatened to blow his brains out if he did not depart at once. That was the nearest Betty had been to receiving a proposition. She looked at the door now and saw three men enter, the one in the middle coming right up to her and saying, Okay, miss, make us three steaks with French fries and some coffee, and make 'em quick. He had an aggressive manner and looked sharply about him as if he expected to be ambushed. Still, he was civilized compared to her brother George, and his companions did say something about getting to Chicago. She busied herself with making the food. The three men stood by the counter, one of them obviously a little nervous. Just then the news came on the radio, which had been playing soft music, and the newsman announced that the notorious bank-robber and killer, Gilbert Lumsden, had escaped together with two other convicts. When the newsman announced the name of the town where the jail was located, Betty dropped the steak she was carrying from the ice-box to the range and gasped, for it was the town a hundred and twenty miles away, less than two hours drive from the diner, where she had twice gone dancing on Saturday nights. She picked up the steak and looked at the man who had given her the order. He was looking at her.

—Okay, so you know, the man said. Gilbert Lumsden, yeah, that's me. Anyone here got anything against me?

—How do you want your steak, Gilbert? Betty asked. Medium rare?

—Make it well done, Gilbert said. And don't call me Gilbert. It was my father's crazy idea of a Christian name, he fancied himself as an opera-lover. My mother always called me Jimmy, and that's okay with me.

I was passed a note on which was written in a small hand, the letters compressed together: Not too promising. Situation too predictable, moral direction obvious. No doubt new characters will be introduced. Perhaps a rich man and his mistress, driven by a chauffeur, confronting the misery of being together without the context of every day life from which their romance was an escape. The usual parallel between the convict fugitive and rich-man fugitive, the escape toward life and the flight from life. Existentialism is always a useful prop in such affairs. Gilbert can take the rich man's mistress as hostage, she, realizing her rich lover is a coward, can fall in love with Gilbert, the chauffeur can surprise everyone with the usual surprises. Or someone else can enter. Perhaps some eccentric, an English novelist or poet, why not? A penniless fool hitch-hiking across the land. Pursued by no one but himself pursuing visions. Will make nice contrast with Gilbert. He could talk poetically while Gilbert hammers out his pseudo gangster phrases. Impress middle-aged ladies, at least. Ending obvious. Police close in. Betty in love with the English poet. Betty held hostage. English poet saves her but gets bullet through his head for his pains, quotes Sir Philip Sidney while dying in Betty's arms. Various obvious possibilities. Just take out the cards from the pigeon-holes and shuffle them. No. Decidedly of no promise. Though of course everything depends on style. On performance.

At the end of the note was the initial H, seeing which I smiled to myself. The old bugger was watching everything. I left the building since the police had already closed in and there was nothing I could do, and went to the car-park where Rosemary was waiting in the Buick. We circled round the clover-leaf and got on the interstate, going west. We drove four hundred miles in less than five hours and I couldn't even tell if I was still awake.

—Why don't we drive on a little farther, Rosemary said.

—Hell, I'm tired, I said.

—But there's nowhere to stop here, she said. Let's at least get to a motel.

—There's room enough in this wagon.

—But, Walt, I'm the one who's doing the driving. You can go to sleep if you like.

—No, even the motion wears me out.

—Well, I should have stayed on the interstate. It was your smart idea to get off it ten miles back. And now where's the goddamn road, I ask you, there's not even a rut here for one to follow.

—So, why do you keep on driving?

—To get the hell out of here, that's why.

—But maybe we're already on your land.

—This? she cried, waving an arm. What can you do with this, enter into business with people manufacturing hour-glasses?

—You knew what to expect, I said. Maybe it isn't. I don't know. We might have made a mistake. If we'd gone on along the interstate, we'd have found two hundred miles later that we should have taken the turning which we took and of course by doing what we have done, taking the turning, it has to turn out that we should have proceeded on the interstate for another two hundred miles. And now if we turn back we won't find the loop to the interstate and if we continue we'll probably lose the last chance we do have of turning back to get on the interstate. That's the way with alternatives, you find yourself landed with the wrong one each damn time.

—Walt, what are you talking about?

—Just putting words together. I'm confused, sweetie, confused. I told you, I'm tired. My head's turning, if you want to know.

—I guessed that, she said.

—Look, I said, there's a cabin there. Let's pull up to it.

—Okay, she said. Looks kind of neat. We could have a good life out here, Walt, a little cabin, desert flowers and all this land around us.

What had looked like a cabin from a distance turned out to be a small house with a faded sign upon it which said Pine Courts. There was a door marked Office and entering it we discovered it to be a family room with shag carpeting on the floor, a couple of plastic-covered sofas, a TV which was on and showed a cowboy in a blue shirt walking down a street his hand ready to draw, but the sound had been turned off so that the image appeared meaningless to anyone momentarily glancing at it. There was no one in the house, however, we soon discovered when there was no answer to our calls of Anyone home? There was a neatly furnished bedroom with another TV which too carried the silent image of the cowboy though his shirt appeared to have turned green and he had walked several cautious steps closer to the saloon for which he was obviously headed. There was a sparklingly clean bathroom next to the bedroom with clean white towels and small cakes of soap. We found another TV set in the kitchen and had apparently missed the crucial action for now the cowboy was on horseback and was riding across a rocky barren landscape at two hundred

79

miles an hour. Rosemary idly flicked the volume switch up and immediately slapped it down on hearing the deafening sound of four thousand violins. A vast refrigerator dominated the kitchen, and we discovered that its capacious freezer was filled with huge cuts of beef. The cupboard below the wet-bar was well stocked with liquor, and we poured ourselves some vodka and sat down to a quiet drink in front of the TV in the family room. There was a cop car tearing around the streets of Los Angeles and since turning up the volume only produced sounds of tires squealing and sirens screaming, we kept the sound off and just watched the silent spectacle of people leaping across dangerous space, a helicopter hovering over a high rise and relaying messages to a cop car which braked, reversed and continued to go berserk through the streets, the detectives speaking into the radio and a motor launch cruising lazily upon the Pacific receiving the message, revving up its engines and, its bow lifted and the wake behind it widening, racing away in the direction of Hawaii. Children went hopping through a park, picking up trash.

Rosemary went and fixed a dinner of two huge grilled steaks and baked potatoes. We sat eating at a picnic table at the back of the house where there were two pots with dead geranium plants in them. The sun hadn't set yet but was not far from the horizon and was beginning to redden and turn the western sky pink.

—This is quite something, Rosemary said.

—It is, I said.

—We are, she began to say something but decided her mouth was too full and did not continue.

—This sure is something, I said.

When she had eaten she leaned back, stretching her arms and taking a deep breath, and looked entirely content.

Just then the sun dropped below the horizon, and very soon darkness fell and stars began to appear. We went to the bedroom and fell asleep, the soundless TV continuing to flicker its images of violence, lust, and small talk in the darkness.

The next morning I awoke with the first light of dawn and went to the kitchen to make some coffee. I made myself a cup and went to the family room to sit down and drink it and to watch the morning news on TV. I was just about to lower myself into the sofa, with my eyes on the screen which showed an Israeli air-raid over a Palestinian camp in Lebanon, when I realized that there was someone there. I withdrew with a start, spilling some of my coffee, and a voice said, Hi there, Walt!

An old man had been lying on the sofa and now raised himself, smiling.

—Excuse me, I said. I didn't know anyone was here.

—That's okay, pal, the old man said, sitting up. Ya'll sleep well? That's a good bed there, huh, had it shipped from Sears in Albuquerque. The name's Hank Howarth, he added, rising from the sofa and offering me a hand.

—How did you know my name? I asked.

—Checked your driver's license, he said. Sorry, Walt, I had to go through your pockets, but I didn't want you to wake up on 'count of me. I didn't want no strangers in the house, see, so I thought I'd get acquainted. If I know a guy's name, I don't care what he does. Why, if I had a pretty young gal in the house as a wife and you said to me, Hank, you said, you mind taking a trip out into the desert and leaving Lou Anne to me for a couple of days, I'd say sure, pal, you just go ahead and give her softies the rub-up, I'll go take me to the Rockies, you just go right ahead and trace your stiff tongue around Lou Anne's nippliloos, that's the way she likes it.

—Oh, come on, Hank, I wouldn't want to do that!

—Sure, you wouldn't, Walt, you're kinda shy with women, and 'sides Lou Anne left me a long time ago, so there's no more chance of it happening than the Lord's blessed green grass growin' out there in the yard. But it's a 'pothesis to think of, I'd say, like every situation in life, a way of measuring, I'd say, how far you'd go with a guy. I'd go all the way, I tell you that straightaway so we know where we stand.

—If I'd known this house was lived in, I said, we wouldn't have taken the liberty. I don't know why we thought it was deserted, but we did. Maybe with all the TV sets on, we shouldn't have.

—Don't mention it, Walt, he said. The house ain't mine, not really, and 'sides I expect to die at any moment so it'll be good to have someone around to dig my grave.

81

—I wouldn't want to dig anyone's grave, I said.

—Sure, I preeshate that, pal, he said. But you don't have to, just close my eyelids and put me out there in the sun, it'll do as well.

—I know it's probably not too delicate to talk about it, but what have you got?

—Nothing terminal or anything, just a feeling I'd be dying any moment. I feel fine, as a matter of fact. Had a good day yesterday, went driving out in the desert, felt just great going round in a wide circle across the white sand. But there's no doubt about it, I'll die any moment. But this house, Walt, as I was saying, it's not a house, it's part of the office and the manager's living quarters of a motel they were building here many years ago when, just after they'd begun, the federal government put through the plans for the interstate, and so this part of the world was abandoned. People just gave up and left. I was one of the construction crew, and I thought I might as well stay here since I'd put the plumbing in.

—But Lou Anne was with you at the time, I said. She was a pretty red-haired girl from Norman, Oklahoma, and she'd come to work as a receptionist and hoped that one night an oil millionaire would be leaving the bar and stumbling across the lobby would need her assistance. Look here, Lou Anne, he'd say drunkenly, ah can't find mah goddamn car keys and that there golden-colored convertible eight point two liter Cadillac El Dorado is no damn good to a guy without a goddamn key. Why, Mr. Wes Cullum, Lou Anne says to him, let me search your trouser pockets for you, and her dainty fingers feel the silk lining of the pockets where she succeeds in making his resolve harden instantly, so that he says, Look honey, just call me Waes, and look sweetie, just forget about the key, ah'll buy another car tomorrow but we could maybe hire this motel for tonight, just you and me together, eh, honey?

—Sure, Lou Anne planned on a millionaire, Hank said. And the first time I met her, I happened to say, Look, Lou Anne, it's been swell talking to you but I've got to go and look at my well. Her eye-lashes fluttered, and she thought that she'd found her oil millionaire and she said, Maybe we could spend some time together, and I said, Sure, why don't we do that right away, the

82

well can wait, and so we did just that. And when it was over, I said, I've got to get to that well, Lou Anne, if I don't there won't be any water for you to shower this evening. WATER? she shouted. Sure, I said, what's the matter? Christ, I thought you'd meant an oil-well. Shit no, I said, I dont' know of no oil-well, but there's a well out there that's supposed to supply water to the motel and I've got to fix it, see, because I'm the plumber.

—But she liked you, I said. You had style in those days, and she stayed when everyone had gone.

—Yeah, he said and added, looking at Rosemary who'd just entered, Hi there, Rosemary.

—So, it was you, she said, looking at Hank. I wasn't dreaming.

—Sure, it was me, he said.

—What are you two talking about? I asked.

—In the middle of the night, Rosemary said, when I was fast asleep, too. There was a figure leaning over me, like a doctor standing by one's bedside, only this guy had lifted up my nightgown and was looking at the riverside prospect where the vegetation is thick beside the thin rivulet.

—What language, Rosemary!

—What were you looking for, she asked Hank, my driver's license?

—I just didn't want a couple of men in my bed, he said. I was just making sure.

—I don't want a couple of men in my bed either, she said, don't you forget that, Hank.

—We'll see about that, he said. Let me fix you some breakfast first. Would you like some steak? Or just some eggs, or some cereal maybe?

—I'll have some orange juice, Rosemary said, a plate of ham and eggs, some toast and grape jelly and some freshly made coffee. Don't just heat up what Walt made an hour ago.

—Okay, Rosie, Hank said, going off to the kitchen like one who's delighted to be of service.

—And, Walt, she said, why don't you go run a hot bath for me? Clean the tub first. And don't run any cold water in it, only hot water. Let me know when it's cooled to ninety-eight, okay?

The bath was ready when the breakfast was, and so Rosemary, dropping off her dressing-gown right there in the middle of the living room and stepping out of her slippers, walked slowly and provocatively toward the bathroom, looking back in too obvious a gesture of a temptress and saying, Hank, put the breakfast on a tray and bring it to me, will you?

Hank was an old man and I figured that while such flirtatious ass-wiggling might bemuse his fancy, Rosemary could expect nothing from him than the gratification of having cruelly teased him. The game bored me, and I went out for a walk. The desert surrounded the house, white space in the harsh morning light in every direction and since it made no difference which way one went, I just walked in a wide circle around the house. Two facts about Hank had put me on my guard. I had learned to suspect alliterative names as fake more often than not: anyone who called himself Hank Howarth could possibly be using an alias. And the story of Lou Anne had clearly been fabricated to lend that credence to Hank's reality which could be discoverable only in absurdity.

I walked for an hour and returned to the house to find Rosemary lying on her stomach on the bed and Hank massaging her naked back. I went to the kitchen and made some coffee and drank a couple of cups. In the meanwhile, Rosemary had dressed herself in a flowing white gown and wore a string of pearls around her neck. The robe hung loosely about her and yet it defined her figure to perfection. She directed Hank to move a sofa so that space could be cleared in the room and sat down, clapping her hands as if to indicate that whatever was about to happen may now begin. Hank switched on the volume of a record-player on which some music was already playing. He began to tap-dance in the space he had cleared. A clown in baggy pants trying to balance himself on a jogging machine would have been more graceful.

—Jesus, Rosemary! I cried. Do we have to spend our time with such nonsense?

—You come here, Walt, she called, waving an arm, come and sit here beside me.

I went and sat next to her on the sofa. Hank was dancing away with a silly grin on his face. Rosemary held my hand and slid down a little in the sofa, indicating with a smile and a nod of her head that she was enjoying Hank's performance.

—Rosemary, I said.

She did not look at me but instead slowly drew up my hand and placed it upon her right breast inside the gown, her eyes still upon Hank and still smiling.

—Oh, shit, Rosemary! I said, drawing my hand away.

She turned her eyes away from Hank's imbecilic dancing, leaned toward me and putting her hands to my shoulders pressed me back, kissing me on the mouth with a considerable pressure. I was about to push her back when she took her mouth away, stepped up on the sofa upon her knees, stretched up, pulling away the front of her gown, and had an exposed breast pressed against my face. All this she did in an instant and I had the uncomfortable feeling of having my nose a little squashed against the soft flesh of her breast before I succeeded in asserting myself and pushing her back. She fell to her side of the sofa and I saw her pulling her gown about her and heard her mutter, Christ, Walt, you could cooperate for once! At the same time I saw that Hank, who had come within three feet of us, had both his hands tightly clasped in front of his pants and was tapping away with his feet with frenzied energy. His eyes had a manic look about them, too. I leaped up at him, held him by the collar, and said, Okay, you lousy pervert, what's the goddamn deal?

He threw his head back, crying Oh, oh, oh!, his eyes shut, and as he cried I saw into his mouth and noticed that his teeth had been stained by cigar-smoke. I let go of him and he collapsed as if he had no more life in him and fell to the ground with a thud, his hands still at his thighs, his eyes still shut, and his mouth still crying Oh, oh, oh!

—Aw, shit, let's get out of here, Rosemary said, rising and going to the bedroom to collect her things.

When we left, Hank was still on the floor, curled up and breathing heavily. Rosemary took the wheel when we drove away.

—All right with you if we head for Denver? she asked.

—Any place that's civilized, I said. Okay, what was that all about? Don't bullshit me either, for I've guessed a thing or two. You'd arranged for us to be in that place, hadn't you?

—Oh, come on, Walt, it was your idea that we turn off the interstate where we did.

—Yes, but if I hadn't suggested it, you would have done so yourself and given me some reason. It just happened to suit you better that I suggested the turn-off.

—That's ingenious, she said. You can explain anything the way it fits in with your idea.

—Sure, scientists do it, too. But in this case, I don't have a goddamn idea. You tell me what the idea was. Who was Hank Howarth? That wasn't his real name, was it?

—How should I know what his real name is? she said. I don't even know the real names of Marilyn Monroe, Ruth Roman, Rosalind Russell, Greta Garbo, Greer Garson and Maria Montez. In any case, you saw him before I did.

—Cut the crap, Rosemary, will you! I know damn well that he knew you.

—What gives you that idea? she asked.

—Item: he told me a story about Lou Anne which was plain bullshit. Item: he declared that he was a plumber when you could tell from his hands that he hadn't held a screw-driver in his life. Item: he said he knew my name because he'd gone through my pockets to check my driver's license. As it happens, my driver's license is in my wallet, and my wallet is in my brief-case since I don't happen to be wearing a coat and there are insufficient pockets in one's pants to keep bulgy things. So, I figured the only way he'd know my name would be from you. And another thing. What was that crap just now of putting on a sex act in front of him? What kind of a deal was that?

—Aw, forget it, Walt, will you? she said. Let's get to Denver and eat some German food.

—His name isn't Hank Howarth, right? I persisted. He's old enough to be your father, right? Shall we say, old enough to be your father-in-law? But, of course, you're divorced. Okay, Rosemary, you don't have to tell me, but I figure that he was Jay Rosenquist's father, old man Marvin Rosenquist.

Rosemary looked at me in a startled sort of way and confirmed my guess which had been more a random conjecture than any logical conclusion.

—Okay, I said, don't tell me what the deal was. I can guess that, too. While he let you have the house in Florida and the oil in Oklahoma to settle his idiot son's divorce he wouldn't let you have the land in the desert unless you played a little game for him first, right? He wanted to see you stretched out there on the floor where he was tap dancing like a maniac, right? And he wanted to see you being screwed while he hopped there like a stupid bear, right? Is that why you pulled me over and stuck your booblette across my face? What was the idea, Rosemary, to give the old man a cheap little thrill for his money? So that his shrivelled up skin might tauten a little? Is that what you were up to? Come on, sweetie, what was the deal?

—You're out of your mind, Rosemary said. If he had been Marvin Rosenquist, you'd have recognized him straightaway since you saw him at the wedding.

—I saw a guy who wore the costume of the Lord Mayor of London with a long curly wig on his head, and this guy this morning was made up to look like a retired plumber.

It was night when we reached Denver. We checked in at a motel, showered, had hamburgers and beer sent to the room and consumed them while watching a talk show on TV before going to sleep. In the middle of the afternoon that day, while driving through the desert, Rosemary had stopped the car and, putting her head to the steering wheel, had wept.

I had walked out to stretch my legs and looking back up the narrow track through the desert had seen a car stopped on the horizon. The driver in it must have seen me look at the car, for just then he reversed and silently dropped back below the horizon, leaving behind a little shimmering haze where the car's hot engine had idled for a moment. There was a boulder to the side of the road, a great hunk of whitish rock conspicuously standing out in that bowl of sand. I took a can of spray-paint from the trunk of the car and wrote on the rock in letters that the driver of the following car was bound to see: WELCOME TO THE

DESERT, H. I thought of adding a Latin epigram but decided it might be obscure or meaningless for my reader and so began writing a line from an English poem which everyone knows but ran out of space on the rock after I'd written LOOK AT MY WORKS, and left it at that, having no choice, thus possibly creating a greater confusion.

The track in the desert finally led to a narrow road and that to a divided highway. Cactus and sage appeared in the sand, and with the land rising steeply, we were suddenly driving through a pine forest and then sweeping down a series of bends with plowed brown earth coming up to the road in triangular sections. Hulme should like this, I remember saying to myself just before Rosemary asked me to pass her a car-sickness pill, It's these bends, she said.

VI

Dialogue With Hulme

Memo to H.: You saw it yourself in the Petrified Forest. The story can develop complications, twists, surprises, while pursuing the mule's-track of clichés down the narrow ravine of public taste, though I admit this mode of expression is degenerate to say the least. You predicted the alternatives, those terrible bifurcations in the mind that the New England hack, R. Frost, wrote a rustic-voiced poem about. The hoe and the hay, but nothing to say. However, you might want to investigate the what else and the unspoken but heard and the not there but seen, for there's this other dimension surely without which there wouldn't be sparkle in water or haze above the sand of the desert.

Many years ago Mario Rodrigues had helped Tom Whittaker and his men drive out the Indians from the country, two-thirds of which now formed Tom Whittaker's ranch, the other third being sold to an insurance company in Dallas with permission to develop the area into a manmade lake with select residential estates upon its shores, the development to be called Comanche Shores in honor of the Indians who had vacated the land. Mario Rodrigues had come from San Luis Potosi, riding on a stolen mule, having heard that the largest ranch across the river at Eagle Pass was at war with the last of the Indian tribes which had not accepted a sober, sheltered existence on a reservation west of the Colorado.

The Indians had fought with bows and arrows, as usual, although they had guns which they had inherited from a tribe in east Texas who had purchased them from a Frenchman from New Orleans and been themselves decimated, abandoning the forests of east Texas for the wide plains of the Valley and gradually being pushed west toward the drier land. Well, sir—Mario was fond of recounting the story of his youth—the Indians, they wanted nothing with guns, they was bad medicine, so they came like they knew how in the old warrior days, and old Colonel Wit, that's Tom Whittaker, that's what we called him in those days, old Colonel Wit, he said, Well, we gotta make it like they know how it is, and so he had us fetch wagons, fifty of them, and had us place the wagons in a circle like the Indians had known in their history and he had us put a bunch of dummies made of rags and sawdust right there in the middle of the wagons, and sure enough the goddamn Indians went screaming for them. The old Colonel laughed and said, See them sons of bitches? It just shows, he said, you've got to fulfil people's expectations in this life or they won't know where the hell they are, you've just got to make the world look like the way people think it is even if you make it with rags and sawdust.

You see, the Indians weren't dumb or anything, they knew the wagons was a trick, but it pleased their imagination to be fighting like in the old days and maybe once they made the charge at the dummies they forgot everything else and just went crazy screaming and yelling when their arrows hit the wagons. That's what human memory does for you, drives you insane. We just picked 'em one by one and shot 'em like sitting ducks, Mario used to say, it was easier than aiming at empty cans in the back yard.

When it was all over, they found a five year old Indian boy beside a creek. Old Colonel Wit decided to adopt him and got the county to pay two thousand dollars a year from federal funds to the Whittaker ranch for the keep of the boy. They gave him the name Shallow Creek, and when he grew to be a man, he came to be known as Chief Shallow Creek, thus pleasing the local population that it had had the magnanimity to bestow a title upon an orphaned Indian while at the same time giving the community the satisfaction of calling the miserable misfit Shallow.

Mario hadn't wet his ass for nothing, swimming across the Rio Grande on an icy February morning with a norther blowing. When Colonel Wit began to organise his ranch and parcelled out two thousand acres along the river for citrus plantations, he got Mario to hire labor, making it worthwhile for the border guys to be playing poker during one half-hour on a certain night so that Mario could move a herd of eager Messcuns to the greener pastures of the U.S.A. Mario brought back a woman for himself, too, young Luisa of the brown eyes and the slow talk. That was okay with Colonel Wit who, as the local rhyme inevitably went, didn't give a shit. The land was cleared, irrigation canals dug, the citrus trees planted and Mario became the boss of two hundred laborers who in the course of time acquired wives, children and beat-up old Ford pick-ups in which to drive to the beach at Port Isabel on Sundays. In the meanwhile, Chief Shallow Creek put feathers on his head and hung about the county seat, sitting mainly in bars which had a color TV, and charging tourists a dollar for a picture, always striking a ferocious pose, his forehead frowning and eyes bulging, his arms folded across his chest, and when the camera had clicked, laughing loudly like someone who enjoys his own joke. The middle-aged ladies in their orange and white pant suits, snapping their Polaroid cameras in Shallow Creek's face, always declared, when waiting for the picture to develop, that he looked the image of Jeff Chandler in the part of Geronimo, and the kids, hearing that, always ran away, screaming.

One day I had a call from Jerry Biderman in the Washington office asking me to go and see what the trouble was in Whittakerstown. I was in San Antone at the time, having flown down from New York on an invitation from the city to judge a beauty contest held as the climactic event of an ethnic festival that aimed to show the city's great diversity of population. I was working hard staring at the girls as they walked up and down the platform, trying to figure out how to compare the beauty of girls whose backgrounds were so varied as Swedish, British, Polish, German, Lebanese, Mexican, Czech, Indian when the call came through.

—Look, Jerry, I'll call you back, I'm busy right now.

—What're you doing, Walt, staring at girls? Jerry asked jokingly, and I said, That's precisely what I'm doing.

—Oh, come on, Walt, Jerry said, don't you ever give up?

—Well, this is a favor, I said, I'm doing the city.

—Sure, it's a favor, you're still the ail-American kid, ready to offer your prick in the service of the nation.

—Not at all, Jerry, I said. Jesus, you do jump to the wrong conclusions.

—Okay, okay, Jerry said, no need to get excited, I understand your predicament, all those nubile sextettes and poor Walt can't even get his finger . . .

—Oh, for chrissake, Jerry!

—Well, call me back when detumescence has set in, but remember this business is more urgent than your infantile fantasies.

I returned to the beauty contest, and decided that I couldn't give the crown to the Mexican girl since it would be too obvious a Caucasian gesture to suck up to the city's large Chicano population, nor to the Lebanese girl for that would offend the Jewish community which originated from Germany, nor to the German girl since, well, I decided to give the crown to the British girl since the British have easily entered into a spirit of compromise with everyone else. I placed the crown upon her head reciting the verse

> Let the British know that although
> Upon them the sun now sets early
> There's still a light out in the west
> That shines from a British girlie

which the San Antone newspapers the next day erroneously attributed to Rudyard Kipling.

I went and called Jerry Biderman after I had spent twenty minutes reassuring the mayor Mr. Johnny Johnson Valdez that my decision was based upon sound aesthetic principles and not governed by considerations of racial harmony in his city, but the mayor said, What were you lookin' at, Walt? The Mexican girl had a pair even a father would be proud of but the British girl, Jesus, Walt, all she had was a coupla tea-bags! What are you, a goddamn purist, or something?

—Look, Mr. Valdez, I began, but he interrupted me with, Call me Johnny, okay?

—Okay, Johnny, it's not just a matter of size.

—Ho, ho, he laughed aloud, it's not a matter of size he says, he said as if to a third person although there was no one else present, oh, come on, Walt, what can you do with a flat-chested girl, it's like trying to ski in Kansas in the summer.

We were interrupted by an elderly lady dressed in a pink gown and having more diamonds about her body than a leopard has spots. She walked shakily up to the mayor and said in a thin but sharp voice, Look here, Sam, what's the city council doing about the dogs knocking over the trash-cans every Sunday night?

I took the opportunity to leave and, returning to my hotel, called Jerry.

—This is a fine time of the day to be calling me to tell me the result of a beauty contest, Jerry said.

—But you wanted to tell me about the trouble in Whittakerstown, I said.

—What did you get on the mayor? he asked.

—What do you mean?

—The mayor, Johnny Johnson Valdez.

—What was I supposed to get on him? I asked. I thought he was a ripe turd. And his name isn't Johnny Johnson Valdez either.

—What's that?

—The mayor's name, it isn't Johnny Johnson Valdez. It's Samuel Murchison, he's pretty sharp. He got Aerolineas Mexicana to schedule a direct non-stop flight from Mexico City to San Antone at eleven a.m. on Tuesdays and Thursdays.

—What's so hip about that? Jerry asked, using an adolescent word to impress me that he wasn't out of touch with this world.

—An Air France 747 lands in Mexico City at ten a.m. on Tuesdays and Thursdays.

—So, what's the big shit?

—Jerry, do you have to talk like a radical of the sixties? You know that outdated jargon offends my ear.

—Okay, okay, proceed with information.

—Well, there seems nothing in the connection until you discover that there's an Air France Caravelle that lands at Orly from Marseille an hour before the 747 takes off for Mexico City. How about that, Jerry?

—Good work, Walt.

93

—Okay, so what about Whittakerstown?

—Get there first thing tomorrow and see what Mario Rodrigues is up to and what the deal is with Chief Shallow Creek.

—What's the connection?

—That's what we want to find out, Jerry said. Then there's Tom Whittaker who rides about on his ranch in a green El Dorado Cadillac, old Colonel Wit they call him. Give him the once over. And, Walt, keep away from the Mexican women, they'll drive you crazy with their large, black eyes.

The line went dead before either of us put the receiver down, and I realized that Colonel Wit had more power in the state than I would, on casual acquaintance, have suspected him of possessing.

I went down to the bar which was designed to look like the economy class section of a 747, stewardesses in light blue with brass wings upon their lapels walking up and down the aisles in a swaying sort of a gait as if the plane were going through turbulence. I took a seat next to a man who had put a newspaper over his face and gone to sleep. The stewardess came, a row of shiny teeth, sparkling eyes and turned-up nose, and asked if I wished to rent ear-phones for the inflight movie. I noticed then that there was a screen up at the front on which a '39 Buick was chasing a '38 Ford on a winding road in the Rockies, an arm out of a window of the Ford firing a pistol at the pursuing Buick and the barrel of a machine-gun coming out of the Buick's side and firing at the Ford and the rock on the side of the road being blown to bits, and I said to the stewardess, No, thanks, honey, just bring me a tequila solo. I put a pillow behind my head, pressed a button to push back my seat and relaxed with the drink.

After the third tequila, I dozed off, the soft piped music having the effect of a lullaby. The man next to me must have shifted in his sleep, for the newspaper fell off his face on to me, waking me with a start.

—Oh, excuse me, he said, taking the newspaper back and folding it.

I noticed then that his face was familiar, the pink complexion, the drooping moustache belonged to a distinct memory, and I said, Haven't we met before?

—The name is ... Humble, he said, pausing before pronouncing the name with a rather forced emphasis. Your humble servant Humble, he added, laughing slightly.

—From Houston? I asked. Oil, obviously?

—What is obvious must surely have a foundation in truth, he said, his eyes narrowing as he smiled, the moustache being uplifted like wings being flexed.

—You travel much? I asked.

—Constantly.

—The inspector ... how shall I put it ... *self-appointed inspector of snow storms and rain storms* . . . a not too awkward a way of putting it?

—It shows a literary bent, a predilection for the elliptical phrase, but it will suffice. We must understand each other somehow.

—Establishing connections, is that it, the general business?

—Observation first, he said. Otherwise, how else?

—I see.

—Precisely.

—And those paintings in the rooms, the sculpture in the patio?

—Exaggerated value. Would you pay ten thousand for an abstract?

—It's an idea!

—I don't know.

I realized that he was intent on remaining inscrutable and so said, You're an Englishman with a tradition of common-sense.

—An Englishman! he spoke as if the notion were irrelevant, and then, closing his eyes for a moment, came up with a neat subterfuge: *here he stands on a larger portion of the globe.*

—*Oh, this is a good country!* I too was familiar with his source, and added: At least we possess a common speech.

—It's a comfort to think so, he said.

On the screen there were four men in a room, hats on their heads, double-breasted suits that made them look barrel-chested, wide ties, and a blonde whose lips quivered nervously. One of the men had been shot in the left shoulder. The stewardess, walking past, saw me staring at the screen and asked, Would you like to rent ear-phones?

—No, thanks, honey, I said, I know the story.

She adjusted the pillow at my head, so that for a moment the brass wings at her lapel were next to my eyes and I inhaled the perfumed odor of her bosomettes.

—It's an interesting story, too, I said to my companion after the stewardess had gone. Full of implausibilities as usual but most absorbing.

He nodded his head, his eyes closed, and said: Whatever holds the attention, passes the time.

—Imagination's everything, I said. What goes on is incredible. And the beautiful thing is that time which we have to pass doesn't exist.

—Should I have said, Whatever passes the time, distracts?

—Distracts from timelessness, I said.

—But memory, he said.

—The seat of fictions.

A man sitting across the aisle had had several drinks and had reached the stage of making silly comments and asked the stewardess who brought him another drink, Where's this flight going?

—Around the sun, she said, and he laughed uproariously.

The next morning I went to see Johnny Johnson Valdez but was told by his office that the mayor had gone to the federal court where Judge Kendrick was serving deportation orders on a bunch of Mexicans who'd illegally entered the country.

—What's the mayor got to do with that? I asked his assistant, a Chicano named Gutierrez.

—He needs the Mexicans, Gutierrez said.

—What for?

—His real estate business, Gutierrez said. He's developing a subdivision south of here, he's called it Hidalgo Heights, it's made to look like a village in Jalisco, and he needs fifty Mexicans to walk about the main square at night. Just smoking and chatting and scratching their balls like they do back home.

—What do you know about Mario Rodrigues, Gutierrez?

—He's Colonel Wit's man, you know that.

—Sure, but what else do you know about him?

—He controls the migrant labor syndicate, Gutierrez said. He can get a man from Eagle Pass to Bismarck, North Dakota, without any papers. This is a big country, Walt.

—Sure, a man gets a mighty thirst.

Just then Johnny Johnson Valdez came into the office.

—Hi there, Walt, Valdez said, beckoning me to follow him into his office, what are you looking for, an honest face? You won't find it looking at Moonface Gutierrez. That's why I hire him, he tells a neat bunch of lies while I'm out. He's had people thinking I'm in New York selling bonds for the city when I'm at the massage parlor giving my body the much-needed tonic of Rosie's fingertips and forgetting my troubles while she's wiggling her ass or swinging her rosettes right by my mouth. And talking of a dame's hot property, what can I do for you, Walt, I mean you haven't come to repent about last night's choice of Patricia Grierson as the cultural queenie, have you? You see the papers this morning? Flattie Pattie Wins Titty Title said one, you see that, huh? Those guys never spare the irony when they write a story.

—That was nothing, Johnny, I said.

—Nothing, he says, nothing! Look, Walt, you betrayed everything my cock stands for, what kind of a perversion you go in for, huh?

—Oh, come on, Johnny, we have business . . .

—We don't have tits, that's for sure. Okay, what's the business?

—Tell me about Hidalgo Heights, I said.

—You wouldn't see them even if you stood right before them, it's plain you don't have an eye for heights.

—Look, Johnny, are you going to quit being sore about last night or do I have to haul my ass to the D.A. to get my information?

—Okay, what do you want to know?

—Hidalgo Heights.

—I heard you the first time. I don't know what you're talking about.

—Gutierrez said . . .

—Forget whatever Moonface told you. He's a liar. That's his job. He's a professional.

—What about the fifty Chicanos you want to hire?

—That's for a movie, he said.

—What movie?

—Some movie, how should I know what movie? Some guy in L.A. called and said he wanted fifty Chicanos.

—Why should you oblige?

—It's business for the city. If they can get the extras they want, they'll make the movie right here in the Hemisfair Plaza.

—Okay, Sam, I said.

—What did you say?

—Sam. Okay, Sam.

—The name's Johnny, he said. What are you trying to do, pretend you can sniff out something? Or something?

—Oh, come on, Johnny, I'm not the only one who knows you're really Sam Murchison.

—Sure, people call me that. It's one of Gutierrez's lies. It gets everybody confused and people think I'm really some kind of a tough guy, wheeler and dealer kind of a hard politico who's so powerful the guys in Houston and Dallas have nothing on him. It's good quality shit, Walt, that's all there is to it.

—I can smell it for myself.

—And what do you mean by that, you turned-up Yankee nose?

—The border's two hours from here, you're closer to the capital of Mexico than to the capital of the U.S.A.

—Look, Walt, do me a favor. I have a nine year old boy who could use a lesson in geography. He's cute with numbers but if you ask him what he knows about Maine, he'll say it's a downtown street. The kid's sense of the world is confused, and that's an understatement, take it from me.

—Okay, Sam, let's have the numbers, what figures you got on the illegal imms.?

—You're talking to the wrong guy, Walt. I'm the mayor for chrissake, I run the city. What you want is the federal office.

—What's Mario Rodrigues got to do with it?

—There's ten thousand guys named Mario Rodrigues in south Texas.

—You know the one I mean, Sam.

—It's a common name, I wouldn't trust anyone who called himself Mario Rodrigues. You can bet the first turd about to exit your intestines he's some Anglo in disguise. They're always doing that, coming here with a moustache dyed black, sombrero in hand, and saying, Meester mair, I'm-a Mario Rodrigues, but let me tell you, Walt, an Anglo's idea of Mexicans is that they come from Sicily and speak like a bunch of goddamn Hollywood Mafia mugs.

—Okay, I said, let me make it as plain as a tortilla. There's a guy who hustles Mexicans across the border, everyone calls him Mario Rodrigues, what've you got on him?

—Look around you, Walt, you're sitting in the mayor's office. Do you see any paper here, a single scrap? I don't touch the stuff, there's not a single file here on anyone.

—Okay, Sam, you're clean. Say, when do they figure they'll make that movie?

—Soon, I guess. I told the guys they ought to shift Hollywood to down here. We've got all the extras they want. The Chicanos can do Indians, Italians, East European Jews and they're cheaper than the New York Jews they usually get to play Chicanos, Indians and Italians.

On leaving his office, I had a word with Gutierrez. Say, Gut, I said, are you planning to go to the border on the mayor's next trip?

—No, he said, I usually stay here to take the calls.

I had guessed right.

Maria Zaragoza, the receptionist at Rosie's Massage Parlor, had a chocolate brown face to which she had applied a pinkish make-up. There was blue eye shadow above her dark brown eyes, a scarlet, shining lipstick upon her mouth. Her black hair was parted at the middle and combed tautly back and held together in a bun at the nape. She had on a pearl grey satin blouse with buttons at the front that strained a little as the uplifted chicaleetos asserted their pressure and provided the male clientele with a homely reception. Because of the effect Maria Zaragoza had upon visitors, she was known as Miss Electric.

—Morning, Tricia, I said.

—How are you today? she said, turning down the transistor on her desk which had been playing Mexican music. We have a special today, she said, making the speech she had learned for the day, a de-urbanisation program. Allow the girl of your choice to release the evil spirit of the machine from your body, her finger-tips will bring back to you the softness of rose-petals and fill your senses with the odors of Eden, she will re-discover the springs within you that are bubbling with delight, she will show you the beauty that is there in your soul. Have you been walking on concrete sidewalks, sitting behind steel desks, is the morning traffic jam tough on your nerves, does your apartment vibrate with your neighbor's stereo, come let us show you that de-urbanisation means more than being rid of tensions, let Julie or Lizzie, Miranda or Juanita, let one of our lovely angels enfold you in her wings and take you to paradise. A Rosie Special, $25.99.

—Oh, come on, Tricia, I said, you don't have to sell me a goddamn special at this time of the day.

—What've you come for then, Walt? This is a massage parlor, we sell ecstasy, what more do you want in this life of economic ills, political corruption and a disregard for the established institutions? You're not one of those hopped-up feds out to get a free screw early in the morning, are you? This is a clean place, Rosie's is Cosy, that's the motto. A place I worked in in Houston got into trouble because a fed persuaded a girl to do the total range of deviate sexuality by promising her a week in Acapulco and offering her the use of his Neiman-Marcus charge account for a month, and the stupid bitch thought maybe she should oblige and see a bit of the world and what do you know, the son of a bitch taped it all. I never heard such squelching and wet-mouthing in my life, like a gorilla was eating a steak. So, don't you come to Rosie's with ideas. I told you, Rosie's is Cosy.

—No, I have no such plan, I assure you.

—Good, she said. We want our customers to be on the level. Okay, if you don't want the de-urbanisation special, we have a deal for $19.99, Lose Your Blues special.

—Yeah, I know about it, I said. Look, I just came in to say hi to Rosie, you don't have to sell me a special.

100

—Why not? What better way to communicate with another human being than through feeling? Why not take your clothes off, lie on a soft bed and let Rosie touch you with her hands softened with almond oil? Just look at you in that goddamn suit! Where do you think you are, Chicago in January? Who makes clothes that size anyway? Shit, your size in pants must be fifty-six!

—Okay, Rickie, don't give me a hard time, just tell me where I can find Rosie.

—Room four, she said. But you can't get there until you pay.

—But I only want to say hello!

—Sure, but I can't let you go past that electric eye in that doorway unless you've paid. It'll keep the next door jammed unless I put a ten dollar bill in this slot.

—Oh, come on, there must be some other door, don't tell me you put in ten dollars every time you want to go to the john.

—I never go to the john, I have a kidney problem.

—But you know what I mean for god's sake!

—No, I don't. You pay ten dollars to go in and ten dollars to come out, and if you take the cheaper special, I give you a penny change on your way out.

—Rickie, can I use the phone?

—Whom do you want to call?

—Rosie.

—Sure, you can use the phone, but you have to ask me to put you on an internal line and you'll have to pay me a service charge of two fifty, it's cheaper than calling your mother in New Hampshire.

—Why, that's robbery!

—Watch your language, Walt.

—I mean two fifty for a phone call!

—I told you, it's cheap. Have you ever been on a long distance flight where you'd paid three hundred bucks for your ticket and they come along with ear-phones for the inflight movie and say that'll be two fifty and then come along with a drop of liquor in a miniature bottle and say that'll be a dollar fifty, and you say, Why, I only paid a dollar on the flight from Rome, why should it be a dollar fifty, and they'll give you some bull about federal regulations, I.A.T.A. rules, and confuse the hell out of you with facts, they make up all kinds of stories with a straight face. That's life, Walt, one load of shit after another. Jesus, the planet stinks!

—Okay, tell Rosie I called. I'd better go now.

—Why should I tell her that? I've a list of other things that I want to talk to her about and by the time I get through them I won't have the energy to remember anything else. I have my own troubles. You guys come in here, see my brown eyes, red mouth and a pair of chiclets that's a goddamn pain to have to keep uplifted so that you guys might see a splitting vision, and you say to yourselves Here's a Chicana I could screw for a couple of pesos and one stale taco, and what you guys never see is that I have troubles of my own. I can see it in your eyes when you say

Let's dispose-a
Maria Zaragoza
Stuff her enchilada
With a hot cockada

but you guys never see that I have troubles, so what good is this life?

—Okay, don't tell Rosie anything, I'm going.

—Sure, run out of here, don't worry about my troubles, just run away from them, haul your fat ass to the fed building, send a call to Washington and give them a load of statistics and then collapse in the bar and drink tequila solos all night.

—What are you talking about now, Tricia?

—Look, I know your deal. You're on to drugs or illegal imms., one or the other. Rosie won't tell you nothing, all her girls are straight, sure they're all Chicanas but they make the best masseuses, they know how to service the male body, not like your Anglo chicks who just giggle and think all a man wants is to get hold of their titaleetos. No, everyone is native here. You go about talking such shit as ethnic groups and Spanish surnames when the truth is we're all native. Would there be an America otherwise?

—Well, it's been nice talking to you, I said, making to leave.

Just then a buzzer sounded and she threw a switch beside her desk. The door opened and a large man of stocky build walked out of the parlor into the reception room and, nodding to Maria Zaragoza, walked out. I recognized him as the man I'd sat next to in the 747 bar, Humble.

—Have you seen that guy before? I asked Miss G. E.

—Sure, I saw him when he went in. Paid thirty bucks.

—What for?

—He got a discount for wanting both De-urbanisation and Lose Your Blues.

—But have you ever seen him some other time?

—Are you curious or are you wanting information? If the former, let me tell you that in spite of your absurd belief that all females are inveterate gossips, I don't care for vulgar curiosity. And if you want information, it'll cost you two fifty for every ten words, it's cheaper than Western Union.

—I couldn't afford your fluency, Trissie, you'd talk the Chase Manhattan out of funds in one hour. Maybe I was just curious. I've seen the guy before. His name is Humble.

—You're wrong there. It's Helmsley.

—Then I must be mistaken, I said. I thought maybe Humble was checking on something.

—Checking?

—Don't worry about him, he isn't a fed or anything. But I've seen him around trying to work things out. In any case, this guy was Helmsley, you say, not Humble. Okay, sweetheart, adios, thanks for the chat, I'll send you a post-card from Fisherman's Wharf.

—Have a good time in Eagle Pass, she said as I was walking away. I was already opening the door when I heard her say that and I stopped and turned around.

—How did you know I was going south?

—A lucky guess, I guess. By mentioning Fisherman's Wharf, you expected me to say San Francisco, and so I thought of saying Charlottesville, Chattanooga, Nacogdoches while saying to myself he expects me to say San Francisco and I'm not going to be misled by his false clue, and in the meanwhile my mind had thought of saying Laramie, Denver, Taos, and then I said to hell with all that, why leave south Texas, and so I said Eagle Pass.

I walked out and quickly worked it out: Johnny Johnson Valdez had said something to Rosie. Rosie was obviously determined not to see me which is why she had gone to such pains to train Maria Zaragoza to keep me out of the parlor and on being asked why by Maria had probably said something about Eagle Pass.

Down in the cabbage-fields they were on their haunches or on their knees, the baggy-trousered men wearing straw hats and the women in ragged frocks, barefooted. Or in the thousand acre lettuce and tomato farms, hands in the roots, the earth, the clayey squelch of the earth, the brown touch of the land. Or in the ricefields of Texas, transplanting the little green shoots from the waterlogged nurseries into the sprinkler-drenched land, the white clouds high overhead. And the cotton-pickers with the same sky above them from the Rio Grande to the Mississippi, a million fingers plucking at the sun's image in the heat, the eyes trapped in the horizon's haze, slit-eyed, weary. There's sustenance then under the weather's vagaries: moisture but not rain, humidity but not air even when the wind blows like trumpets from the Bible and the chickenhawks rise upon graphic undulations.

The land sucks upon underground waters, draws upon its own depths to grow lush with grass or to turn up moist under the plow, glistening richly with its own dark chemistry. Pastures where the cattle fatten, or farms where pumpkins and watermelons are inflated by the air that blows in from the tropics. Sufficiencies, too, in the weather then, the moisture that nourishes, the humidity that forces openings along the stem. There on their knees, on their haunches, the ballooned soiled frocks, the patched-up baggy pants, and brown hands in the earth moving northward with the harvest, caressing the green that rises from America.

Rosemary called me from New York and said, I simply have to tell you this that Pru Essenfoot just told me about a girl in her office called Teresa who had an affair with a guy called Harry who was Teresa's best friend's, Beatrice her name is, lover. Well, Beatrice—everyone calls her Busy Bee—had a quarrel with Harry and the next thing that happened was Harry and Teresa were seeing each other and getting closer to each other's skin. Teresa is a literary type and has dreams in which she's a sailor being picked up by Hart Crane—shit, don't you have some weirdos in this town! Anyway, Teresa got down to the substance of Harry's fantasies quoting Shakespeare: Where the bee sucks, there suck I.

—Oh, come on, Rosemary, when will you New Yorkers grow up?

—It's literature, Walt.

Trailing Humble, I flew up to Chicago. On the plane, I found the only free seat was next to him and so made a joke of it, saying, Maybe we're still in the bar in San Antone!

—I must say I got a bit airsick in there last night, odd, isn't it?

—I think I'll doze off after I finish this whiskey, I said. I hope you don't mind.

Soon, I pushed back the back-rest and closed my eyes, holding a hand up to my forehead.

Since he sat with his back-rest upright, I could glance at the spiral notebook in his lap on which he was inscribing numbers with a felt-pen.

—Pay it no attention, he said as if to himself, I'm only working out a puzzle to pass the time.

—What's the puzzle, I said, putting a newspaper over my face and stretching my legs.

—If the world population is to rise to x billion by the year 2050 and there are y million Catholics in the world in the year 2000, how appreciably will x be diminished if the Church were to accept contraception from the year 2000?

—Frankly, if I were the Pope, I said, putting the newspaper aside, I'd get me a spot on TV and say, Look fellas, I've been using it all my life.

—Well, he said, I would be a little more careful. The Catholic vote in this country is not easily to be overlooked and one's relations with the territories between Nuevo Laredo and Tierra del Fuego have to be handled with discretion. But it's only a puzzle, an answer will give me a sense of achievement, as when I solve a crossword puzzle, but will make no difference to the world.

—Sure, it's only a puzzle, I said. Anything that's of consequence and might change the world is only of speculative value. If our politics were as serious as the anguished debate of the liberal intellectuals will have them, we'd have anarchy, and similarly if our religions took moral questions seriously we'd all be slaughtered by the zealots. Better the polarity of prejudices, the imbecility of dogma and the idiocy of politics, they keep us running. Dear God, give us this day something to be outraged about so that we can congratulate ourselves on our liberalism.

—I've examined cynicism, he said. The trouble with it is that it rejects phenomena but is not in a position to accept metaphysics. It's a most unsound procedure.

—Art takes of both worlds.

—And therefore cheats, he said.

—Did you know about the Prince who went to Spain and saw Princess Isabella in an orange grove, orange blossom in her hair, a light blue ribbon at her bodice holding up her delicate royalties and fell in love with her? He wrote sonnets to her, sang sweet songs that echoed softly in the orchard where butterflies played in the speckled light, and she too fell in love with him.

—Indeed? I was under the impression the young man had a club-foot.

—It's possible, I said, for the story does develop with Isabella's father receiving an offer for her fair royaltits from the King of France who by an extraordinary chance happens to be the young Prince's father.

—It's inevitable, the Prince has to kill the King.

—But in circumstances in which he does not know his enemy is his own father.

—Yes, I've heard that one, he said. It's too easy, though there might be something to be said for fulfilling expectations. Plagiarism has its uses, but the very attempt sometimes convinces many people of their own originality. Did you not on seeing a great actor, mimic his manner and tone and soon convince yourself that you had some talent, too? That is one of the misfortunes of art, to be burdened by practitioners who mimic.

—Did you hear about the guy who walked about the streets of a walled city . . .

—Thebes?

—Could have been. . . . Looking for a killer? He walked into bars, spent hours at the police station, asked veiled questions in shops, and found himself in the house where the murder took place at the exact time of the murder, pistol in hand.

—For he himself was the murderer. Yes, I've heard that one, too. Fusions of past and present. Very interesting but rather a trick. How can time not pass between pages? As for innovation, it becomes a mannerism as soon as its purpose is perceived.

—So, you don't admit any connections?

—There are possibilities perhaps, but why insist on insights? We've had these stories around for a long time.

—You know when I was a kid and didn't have the advantage of Playboy, I used to spend my afternoons in museums looking at the nudes by Goya, Degas, Rubens, even Henry Moore. Nowadays it's easy, you tear off the center page and go to the bathroom. Or take the whole goddamn magazine with you, and wear yourself out.

—I don't suppose you'd want to waste your time arguing against pornography?

—Why should I? I've nothing against it provided its purveyors don't go about claiming it's art. Filth for filth's sake is okay.

—What about your fourteen-year-old . . .

—I was fourteen myself once and was happy to discover new opportunities to jerk off. With the right hand. With the left hand. With soap. In the ocean. Wrapped in a banana skin. In front of a mirror. Wearing my mother's bra. Looking at the ads in Vogue with all those lovely clothes to take off. Etcetera. And spilling it out on pictures of Rita Hayworth, Susan Hayward, Ann Blyth, Ruth Roman, etcetera. If someone had tried to protect my innocence, I'd have been bored to death.

—It's inescapable, then?

—What?

—That all political, sociological, anthropological, psychological and critical analyses are only rhetoric.

—Of course. Otherwise everything would have been resolved by the eighteenth century, at the latest, probably a couple of thousand years before that, and all intellectual debate would have come to an end for absolutes are absolute and there's nothing more to be said. Personally, I'd blame Euclid, Pythagoras and Aristotle for sending the stone rolling through the mossy minds of system-mongers.

—Abusers of language, would you say?

—We agree on this, at least. Language perceives but jargon explicates. And one might add meanings are communicated through expletives.

—No ideas but in things? Is that it, the poet's way?

—No ideas. No things. No time.

—Interesting, he said. But it's an idea.

—We've had too much philosophy not to have bad habits. All we needed was poetry but we've always conceded it the least relevance. Plato banished the poets not because they were hostile to the republic but because they would have knocked philosophy out of the universe. Language equals vision. But you will have noticed that it's the cunning jargon-mongers who misinterpret the visions who sit in professorial chairs, not the poets. There's no conspiracy, it's only a question of survival: in any complex society the poet appears as a buffoon, by permission.

—If this were universally believed . . .

—Paradoxes now?

—No, I agree all linguistic devices have become corrupt, but in avoiding them we attempt chaste beginnings, like Euclid.

—And thus become trapped in the first paradox!

—Precisely.

—So?

—What we began with. No ideas. No things. No time.

The plane began to lose height and I said, We must be coming up to O'Hare.

—No, we're still over Kansas, he said, leaning toward the window.

Just then the aircraft swung to the left, banking steeply so that from the aisle seat I could see that we were flying over a vast plain of ripening wheat. The jet straightened out again and began to gain height, soon resuming its monotonous flight. I asked a passing stewardess if the pilot was all right and she said, Sure, he's okay, he just gets bored sometimes and likes to play a little game. He just called for some coffee. I always add a drop of whiskey to it, she said, winking at me.

—And yet without art, he said.

—This is an interminable flight, I said. What do you plan to do in Chicago?

—Walk around, look at a few things. See what's going on.

—That's life.

I called Jerry Biderman from the airport. Okay, Jerry, I said, I've tailed him to here, better get some local guy to take over now.

—We already have, he said.

—By the way, Jerry, who is this guy anyway?

—Oh, a new recruit, keen as hell. If you asked him to tail a statue, he'd do it, just stand there in the park beside a tree, a newspaper in front of him, coat collar pulled up, waiting for the statue to make a move. Some guys do nothing that's not right by the movies.

—No, I don't mean him. Humble.

—You mean Hulme?

—Whatever you want to call him. Sometimes I don't know whether I'm tailing him or if he's after me.

—Yeah, he called from San Antone and said that he expected you'd want to catch the same plane and so he'd keep a seat for you. What did you talk about?

—Pornography.

—Good work, Walt!

—But he's not interested in it, he's on to something else.

—Okay, Jerry said. We'll take over from here. You better fly back and resume the Colonel Wit file. I'm sorry we had to get you off that for a day, but there was no one else of your caliber to accompany Hulme. Though it might have had the effect of confusing Colonel Wit, your flying to Chicago when the action is in Texas, even make him think you're after something else.

—When can I take some time off, Jerry? I've to visit Rosemary.

—She can join you in Texas, she needs a vacation. You can take her across the border and buy her some hand-embroidered shirts.

—Okay, Jerry, but I'll need a vacation myself when this is done.

I rode across the dry land on my trusted horse Gary. It was late in the summer and even the wild flowers had lost their color and dried up. It was a hard land with sparse stunted trees that gave no shelter from the sun. There were four figures in the distance and when I was close enough to distinguish them I saw that they were dark men in baggy pants and torn shirts, digging in a heavy, reluctant manner.

—Howdy there, amigos! I called to them.

They looked up at me briefly, wearily, and turning to their task almost simultaneously raised their pickaxes and brought them down sluggishly, the iron points making a hard metallic sound against the rocky soil. I observed that their labor had made no impression on the land. They had penetrated no more than a couple of inches into the soil, and it was not clear what their purpose was. There was nothing around them for miles. They could not have been digging a canal, for there was no water to tap; nor could they have been thinking of putting down some seed, for one wouldn't come twenty miles from a village into the middle of a barren wilderness to do that. I watched them for a few minutes. Slowly and laboriously they raised their pickaxes and let them fall on the land almost as if they'd lost the strength and the will with which to put some force behind the action. One of them stopped digging, held the pickaxe in front of him, leaning on it, and turned to stare at me.

—This country don't give nothing, he said slowly, raising an arm to wipe the sweat from his forehead with a soiled sleeve.

—What are you digging for, I asked jokingly, gold?

The three other men stopped, too, and the four of them stared at me with anger and contempt. Fearful that they might misinterpret my friendly interest as an ironical mockery and be provoked into attacking me, I bid them farewell and rode on. I turned to look at them several times, for there was nothing else of interest in that empty land and we were going slowly since I didn't want to press Gary in that heat. The four remained the same as far as I could see, slowly digging away. I had not observed them possess anything other than the pickaxes, and their torn clothes could not have accommodated a slice of bread or a packet of cigarettes. It was difficult to tell, for I knew the country well and had a fair idea of its population and resources, where they had come from and how they were going to survive.

Rosemary had taken an apartment on Comanche Shores in a complex beside the lake at Whittakerstown. She'd just come in from playing tennis and still had on a white T-shirt and shorts. The exposed parts of her body glistened with sweat and the sun had turned her red. The T-shirt hadn't been tucked into the shorts, giving her a girlish look, and each time she raised an arm the shirt rode up revealing her navel.

—Why don't you make yourself a drink while I shower, she said, kicking the tennis shoes off her feet.

—Did you have a good game? I asked.

—Won in straight sets. There's a wet-bar between the kitchen and the dining area, the drinks are in there. And, Walt, she added, going away toward the bedroom and already pulling off her T-shirt, make me a cool orange juice, and, well, why not, add a jigger of vodka to it. Make that two jiggers. Plenty of ice.

I went to the wet-bar and found the drinks. I decided to have vodka on the rocks myself, and was getting the vodka bottle out when I heard Rosemary say from the bedroom, You'll have to eat alone tonight, Walt.

—Why is that? I asked, turning around and seeing her standing naked in the doorway of the bedroom.

—I've a date. Sorry, but I didn't know you'd be here today.

—Who's the guy? I asked, walking to the refrigerator to fetch some ice.

—A guy who looks the picture of César Romero. The name's Mario Rodrigues. Boy, am I going to screw him!

I made the drinks and sat down, hearing the sound of the shower and Rosemary singing incomprehensibly at the top of her voice. When she'd finished her shower, she walked to where I was sitting for I'd put her drink on a table in front of me. She was still dripping wet and was towelling herself as she walked up to the table giving her droplettes a good rub. She picked up the drink, saying, Do I need this screwdriver!, and walked back to the bedroom, her buttocks rippling behind her.

—You've got a neat pair, Rosemary, I called after her.

—Thanks, she said. I wish I could say the same about yours, but what can one say about a coupla pill-bugs?

—That's okay, I said, I understand.

—Say, she said walking up to the door, wearing a bra but nothing else, did I tell you that Hume called me before I left New York?

—No, I said, looking at her damp crotch, and she went away to return a moment later, having put on pink underpants and begun to brush her hair.

—Yeah, he called the other day and said he'd seen the house in Key West. It isn't worth more than ten grand apparently, and what's ten grand nowadays, you couldn't get a face-lift with that. Some goddamn Cuban family's been living in it since '61 and the whole thing's run down. The Cubans grow bananas in the back yard, and the father does a little fishing, that's how they live, and social security, nothing like a tax sheltered life, I guess. I could have them evicted if the property had potential.

She put her hands behind her and tightened her bra and then pulled the straps up a bit to give her breasts an uplifted, deep-cleavage look and when she presently put on a long white gown the décolleté effect was striking.

—So, I said to him if the Cubans can't afford to pay rent, maybe they can send me a bunch of bananas from time to time, on a regular basis.

—That isn't a bad deal, I said.

—Though you know what I could do, maybe go down there one day, do up the house and live there with the Cubans to attend upon me. I could build them a nice little shack at the back maybe, and it could be a good life.

—Rosemary, where did you meet Mario Rodrigues?

—The handsome Romero you mean? He was in a bar last night, you'd never guess who took me there. Old Colonel Wit himself!

—No!

—Sure. I'll tell you about him in a minute, but there we were in the Bar Camelia and as I walked in holding Wit's arm the first person I saw was Romero, a tequila lifted to his lips. Colonel

Wit saw a rancher he wanted to have a word with which left me free for a couple of minutes in the best tradition of coincidental occurrences. So I walked up to Romero who still had the glass at his lips though he hadn't sipped from it yet for he was watching me walk up to him giving my hips a bumpety-boo and I said, If that's real passion in your eyes, we could meet tomorrow, I'd like to screw you. Maybe we could have dinner first, he said, smiling graciously. Why, that'll be just dandy, I said, bowing a little to give him a sneak preview. So that's what I'm going to do right now, Walt. Eat red snapper veracruziana, drink a whole lot of tequila and screw a Chicano. It's great to be away from New York, believe me.

—What about Colonel Wit? I asked.

—He's a gentleman, Walt. Why, he wouldn't let me budge from his convertible Cadillac until he'd walked round to open my door.

—How did you meet him?

—I had a call from San Antone just before I left New York. A man named Valdez who said he'd been talking to you. He said he'd called Colonel Wit and told him to expect me.

—Why should he do that?

—Colonel Wit wants publicity. He wants to promote this area for vacations and Valdez thinks whoever comes here has to fly to San Antone first, so it's business for his city. They're working on a long weekend deal for New Yorkers, a night in San Antone and two in Whittakerstown that'd take in the Alamo and some goddamn mission in San Antone and fishing and sailing and tennis on Comanche Shores. That's why I'm getting the red carpet, I'll at least get it mentioned in Helen Kreutzer's column and before you can say amigo the women'll be jumping right out of the hair-driers at the beauty parlors to catch the plane. They've had enough screwing Puerto Ricans, anything for a change of style. Maybe it's only a pipe-dream of old Wit's. But that's how provincials are, Walt, they think their part of the world will just about ravish the tourists. Anyway, I'm going to keep quiet about it for a while. I wouldn't want to share Romero with them greedy paws from New York. Not till I've had my fill.

When she'd gone, I took a cool shower, heated up an enchilada dinner and then sat down in my pajamas with some beer and caught up with my paperwork, thinking to myself that Rosemary had walked straight into Colonel Wit's trap. He'd planted Mario where she'd see him first thing in the bar and he'd deliberately got out of the way for long enough for Rosemary to proposition Mario. Mario had known what to say. He'd heard of New York dames and the wild perfumes they wore, and so he'd figured he'd play along with Colonel Wit's proposal without telling the Colonel he had his own reasons, too.

—Okay, Walt, Colonel Wit said when I confronted him with my theory at ten p.m., you come with me and I'll show you what I mean.

—Where to? I asked.

—O just a little drive.

We drove away in his green El Dorado. He pressed a button and the top removed itself silently, and then he thrust a cartridge into the tape deck and a thumping piano and several excited violins began to keep time to the fast speed of the car. The headlamps picked out the deserted street for three blocks, at the end of which Colonel Wit swung the car left in a wide curve, shot up on to a highway, drove down it for two miles in one minute and shot off it on to a dirt road. He slowed down some on the dirt road because the noise of the tires with little rocks knocking in the wheel arches drowned the music. It was a straight narrow road with orange trees on either side, rows of them stretching back from the road far into the darkness. Colonel Wit turned the car right and took a narrow muddy road through the orchard, the trees so close to the car that oranges seemed to be bouncing in the beam of the headlamps. He drove slowly now, switching off the music and dipping the headlamps, so that there was only a slight hum of the tires as they went over the compacted mud. He turned the car twice again through narrower tracks, until we were out on another road of hard, dry mud. He switched off the lights altogether and slowed down to maybe five miles an hour. I could see nothing since the orange trees were all around us. Soon, he switched off the motor and let the car coast for some fifty yards when he gently pressed on the brakes. Saying in a whisper, Take a good look now, he suddenly switched on the headlamps.

There on the edge of the orchard, beside an irrigation canal beyond which was a tomato patch, were a man and a woman on the ground.

From our angle, we saw the white back of the lady who sat astride the man who lay on his back, as if cushioned in mud, his small brown hands at her hips.

We saw the woman's back first, her buttocks going up from the man's thighs and then, in slow motion, coming down again until they flattened out and bulged at the sides as she pressed down upon him, before rising again, slowly, deliberately.

The man's hands moved a little lower from the hips and clutched tightly at her flesh; his legs were stretched out toward us from beneath the woman, his thighs parting and coming together as he attempted to push upward from the small of his back.

Riding up, she strained herself backwards, so that from the side her back and neck must have appeared arched, but we only saw the head straining back until the forehead, nose and chin appeared momentarily in view before she leaned forward and pressed down upon the man again.

In the moment that she leaned forward and pressed down upon the man, he attempted to raise himself, his face coming up toward hers, but she swung her arms up and pushed him back at the shoulders and then put a hand down upon his face, pressing his head to the dirt.

She straightened her back again and rode him slowly, deliberately, asserting the rhythm she preferred.

Then suddenly she speeded up, rising higher and coming down abruptly, tilting back her head and jerking it forward with each rise and downward thrust.

The man raised his legs, moving his hands to clasp her back, straining his thighs to her buttocks, while she beat down upon him, while she leaned forward and pulled up his face to hers in a violent collision, her hands in his black hair, the force of her thrusts at his groin driving him into the dirt the more he strained to rise from it.

When the convulsion had passed, the man's legs went limp and his head fell back.

—She's not through yet, Colonel Wit said, she'll screw him till he has nothing left.

She lifted herself and lay upon him, her legs stretched along his, her hands at his shoulders, her mouth upon his while at the same time her hips and shoulders rocked from side to side, pressing him into the earth with all her weight.

—I could use a drink, Colonel Wit said, driving out of the orchard. We have a whole bunch of recreational projects, you guys are going to forget Vegas by the time we're through. That was nothing. When we get this place organized, we'll put on a show you won't believe. Or ever forget. We've got the men who can take anything. What we need is a whole bunch of dames with blue eyes and lips hotter than a jar full of jalapenos. Only one can win this race.

VII

Other Visions, Other Dreams

Adieu, kind friend; I have no more time to moralise. The sun is hot, and I must on and take my chances. There's a land out there whose voice is the westerly wind. The voyager to Oregon hears it, and takes courage, the trader to Santa Fe hears it, but cannot look up at the broad blades of icy light that gather to a whiteness, having the Platte and the Arkansas to cross with packed wagons. Adieu, my beautiful Kentucky, whose forests have been my home, I must go to a higher land where even the Crow warriors riding home from their hunting grounds have not been. *Forty days I shall travel towards the sun, yet I shall not touch his home—I shall only be in the far West—*

By the time I reached St Louis, the party had already left for Independence. Alone on Gary, I could travel faster than a wagon train but on arriving in Independence I was surprised to learn that the traders had set out the day before. Well, my boy, I said to Gary, every mother's son in the U.S. is born to stand on his own two blessed feet, and I guess the Lord intends for us to make it on our own. And so we rode out for the Platte.

We camped just out of Independence waiting for the grass to grow. It was a retarded spring, ice an inch thick in the bucket outside the tent each morning. April began with a blizzard, turning the world into a frosty Sahara. The sun took solitary possession of the sky two whole days, raided the earth, making the ice run down slopes and gullies. The wind returned, from the south came clouds bearing rain. Now the grass should grow, we said, and already many teams were heading West, entering the unknown of those who have formed no attachment to the place where they have been and are excited only by the possibility of what might be beyond the horizon. But we are prudent, wait for the grass to grow. Forty oxen-drawn wagons go past one day, struggling laboriously through the heavy ground. Men and women sit up front, the ladies all bonnetted and rosy-cheeked in the sharp air, but what brightness in their eyes and how the bosoms rise with the passion that has suddenly filled America! Some eager souls go past on horses, overtaking the wagons in a confusion of kicked-up mud; or on mules that have scarcely been broken and seem intent not only on dislodging their masters but also on flying off in twenty different directions at once. Better, for these, the hardships of the future, the problems that will need attention than the boredom of present waiting.

Back in Independence for supplies, I was caught for half an hour in the traffic of carts, wagons, horses and mules in a muddy street. Everyone was shouting at everyone else and at the animals. Oaths were being vigorously exchanged by the teamsters, tradesmen were calling from their shops or running up to a wagon with offers of buffalo skins at reduced prices. Independence was a town everyone came to in order to leave it.

It gave a man a thirst as big as the Kansas sky just trying to cross the street, and I went into a saloon with the intention of drinking a beer but, once at the counter, asked for a whiskey instead. I wouldn't have minded hearing the barman's opinion of the weather but he didn't have a civil word for me. The bar was crowded and the only time the barman looked at me for more than a second was when I pulled out the billfold, otherwise his eyes were on glasses and bottles or right past me over my head into the smoke of the saloon. In a far corner, on a small platform that served for a stage, a rosey-cheeked portly man with sad eyes and a drooping moustache, waved a hand in the air and said something which I didn't hear. He paused, looked up at the ceiling and said, That is the question. He was the usual kind of actor one saw everywhere, moaning about a question that didn't concern me none, so I quit looking at him. I was on my third drink, standing there with my elbow on the counter, when a bright-faced, clean-shaven guy next to me who was no taller than my shoulder said, his eyes sparkling: Going west, brother?

—Yep, I said, not wanting to give too much away to a stranger.
—California maybe?

—Maybe.

—It's a wild land out there, he said.

—Could be, I said, wiping my mouth with the back of my hand.

—Any women with you?

—Nope, I said.

—Sure, he said, it's a man's business, going for gold, that right, brother?

—Sure is,

—There's women here, he said.

—Yeah?

—Depends on your fancy, he said. Some men like to have a good time before they go into the lonely world out there, in the west, where they're only gold-hungry men. Some men like to take the memory of women with them.

—You making me an offer, mister?

—Some men have nothing to lose, he said, since they're setting out to make their fortune in the west, so they take a woman for the night, get a feel of her body to last them a year maybe.

—Mister, you making me an offer? You got some deal figured out?

—Maybe, he said. Some men like the odor of a woman cling to them for a little while when they ride west on their sweating horses.

—Okay, what's the deal?

—Easy, brother, just take it easy.

—You some kind of a pimp, or something?

—I said take it easy, okay? As I was saying, some men like to hold on to a woman while they're lying out alone under the stars.

—I heard you, goddamnit! Quit the poetry, willya! What's the deal? How much?

—Easy now, brother. Five bucks to me and ten to the lady. You go up the steps there, knock on the second door on your right, it'll be Estelle. Tell her Charlie sent you.

I pulled out five dollars and thrust them at him and was about to walk when he said, Hold on, brother, have a drink first, maybe you'll need it. Be my guest, brother.

He made a sign to the barman to pour us some more whiskey, and I thought he was quite a gentleman, offering me a drink when you'd think all he had on his mind was to lay his greedy paws on my dollar bills.

—Thanks, I said, drinking, I appreciate it.

—You're welcome, brother, he said. Don't think it's the money I'm after, that kinda loose change is nothing to what you guys are going to make when you hit gold. I just like to see you guys go happy. It's good to have a little beauty in the soul, brother.

—Why don't you go west, too?

—It's my leg, he said, I wouldn't make it ten miles west of Independence.

I went up and he called after me: The second door on the right, the name's Estelle, tell her Charlie sent you.

From the staircase, I got a glimpse of the actor in the corner. He had a skull in his hand and was talking to it. I'd seen that trick before. The actor picks up a skull and says Alas! And then something about kissing the guy's lips when he was alive. That's what poetry is, full of weird surprises.

I ran up the remaining steps and found myself in a corridor. The girl in the red chiffon dress who opened the door looked puzzled when I said, Estelle? She simply stared at me with her large brown eyes, so that I said, Your name is Estelle? Eh, baby? She looked me over, her eyes dropping all the way down to my muddy boots and then raised her eyes to stare at my face some more while slightly shaking her head to say no.

—Well, excuse me, I said, maybe I can find Estelle in another room, Charlie sent me.

She didn't move out of the doorway and I took a ten-dollar bill from my pocket to make it clear that I was no mean soul.

—The name's Alice, she said, stepping back so that I followed her into the room, closing the door, saying, Nice knowing you, Alice, Walt's the name.

—Okay, Walt, you can put that piece of paper away and sit down, she said, going to a small table and turning the lamp low, taking a seat beside it herself.

She's okay, I thought looking at her long black hair and those large brown eyes, she'll do just fine, her parsleys are okay too for a little nibble.

—Who's Estelle? I asked, thinking maybe she wanted a little conversation first, she looked pretty lady-like.

—Don't worry about her, she said.

—Sure, I ain't worried about her at all, I said, smiling.

—Okay, she said, what's the message?

—Charlie said to say he sent me.

—Quit the cryptic shit, she said.

—I beg your pardon? I said, a little startled. But Charlie . . .

—I heard you, she said.

—Look, I just gave five bucks to Charlie for this visit.

—Give him another five when you go, if you want to, what do I care?

—You don't have to feel sore about him, he's only doing a job, a lousy job, but it's a job, what with a bad leg and everything.

—You don't have to tell me about some lousy hustler, she said.

—Okay, lady, maybe we don't have to talk about it.

—When do you go? she asked.

—Any day now, I said. Just waiting for some rain.

—The wagon's ready.

—What wagon?

—The wagon.

—Sure.

—You don't have to wait for rain. I'm ready to leave tomorrow.

I got the picture. She was counting on me to escort her west. Well, let her think I was here to help her, she wasn't going to see me again after I'd finished filling up her squishygoo with my squishyglob. My mistake was I didn't even think when she spoke that she might mean more than she said.

—Isn't there a message? she asked, adding when I did not reply immediately: From Santa Anna.

—I don't know the guy, I said.

—Don't you try that on me! she cried. Just because we're a thousand miles from Santa Fe you think you can get away with cheap blackmail! What do you want, that I should give you a stack of dollar-bills, before you open your goddamn mouth, that I should open my legs for you before you give me the message, you dirty stinking cheap blackmailer!

—Lady, I don't understand, I thought you were a pro at it.

—Look, cowboy, she said, just tell me what Santa Anna said and I'll make it up to you, okay?

—Santayana?

—Yeah. What's the message?

—Excuse me, Alice, but tell me why do you think I should be coming from Santa Fe with a message from Santayana?

—Because you asked for Estelle and then waved the ten-dollar bill, you knew the password and the sign.

—That's what Charlie told me to do, I'd never met the guy before, I thought I was going to find a woman up here.

—What did you find, a horse or something?

—Well, you know what I mean by a woman. O come on, Alice, what's all this about?

—You tell me, cowboy.

—Look, lady, I ain't a cowboy, I just happen to be going west because I'm restless, because staying in the same place makes my ass blue with boredom, because there's a big sky out there that I want to be under. It's not just the gold, Alice, that's only an excuse to give the old folks, that's only something to fix your mind on while camping out there in the prairie under the big stars wondering what the hell this country is that drives you crazy unless you're on the move. Okay, so what's the deal with this Santayana?

—I'm waiting for a message from Santa Anna, I've got to get the wagon to Santa Fe, that's all. But I've to know that the trail is clear.

—What would you say if I said there's some misunderstanding? Truth is, I've no idea what you're talking about.

—That's okay, she said, I was only testing you. I never heard of anyone called Santa Anna, I mean what kind of a queer name would that be for a goddamn Spaniard?

—What do you mean, for god's sake?

—I don't know anyone in Santa Fe, I just have a fantasy that I know a Spaniard there named Santa Anna whom I'm going to help with a wagon-load of ammunition. I try that on all the men who come to me, it makes them think I'm some dark woman with a secret life of romance and intrigue. Some get nervous and simply run out, others think it an honor to be with me and pay me more. It's amusing, gives me a sense of dignity. One needs variety in this life, Walt.

—That's just dandy, I said. You'd freeze any man's balls with that kind of talk. How do you expect me to do anything now? Eh, Alice?

—The name's Estelle, she said.

—That's dandy, too. Jesus, don't we have some crazy women in this country!

—Okay, go ahead and strip, she said. Come on, cowboy, just go ahead and start pawing me and tearing off my clothes, let's see where we'll get, I bet yours ain't no bigger than the thimble my kid sister uses when she sews a frockette for a doll. It's all talk and no cock, cowboy.

—You've perfected the technique, haven't you? Attack with words, confuse us, humiliate us so that we just can't do it.

—Ho, ho, so the truth's out, is it? The whiskey's worn off and the illusion of vigor's given way already to disenchantment. You can make it in your dreams, cowboy, you can make it round a campfire talking to men, but you can't make it in bed.

—You do have a way of making a man proud of the women of this country. They'll talk any goddamn shit to feel bigger than a man.

—Walt, she said, changing her voice, giving the irony a sharper edge, I'm just dying to have you make love to me.

—With your verbal foreplay, lady, even a rabbit would lose interest.

—That's swell. Blame me for what you can't do.

—Here's your ten bucks, I said, rising.

—No, honey, I've earned more than that.

—I haven't even touched you, for god's sake!

—Precisely, How would you like the folks of Independence to know you couldn't even make it, that you were too scared to take your pants off?

—Ha, blackmail, is it?

—A girl's got to make up for the disappointments of life, she said. Make it thirty.

—THIRTY!

—Why not? You've had a good time. Not every man gets half an hour with a girl who can match his intellect. Isn't that better than five minutes in bed when, puff, puff, it's all over and you don't know afterwards what really happened and if it was worth anything?

—I don't think you even deserve ten.

—I'm not talking of what I deserve, she said. I'm talking of what you'll pay to save yourself embarrassment. Thirty.

—I don't give a damn about embarrassment, I said. I'm riding out west tomorrow.

—Why don't you take me with you? she said.

—What the hell for?

—Just someone to talk to, maybe. Or if times were bad, I could make money for you.

—I ain't no pimp, lady. And I told you, it's not the money, it's the country. Sure, the gold's on my mind, but it's the country in my soul that's got me so hopped up. You wouldn't ever see that. Here, have fifty bucks, and goodbye.

—Just a minute, Walt, she said, not even looking at the money I'd recklessly put on the table beside her.

—What now?

—Oh, nothing. I just don't want you to leave here thinking bad things of me. The money's not important, you know that. Believe me, I wouldn't be living this life if it was only for the money.

It occurred to me that I should take back the fifty bucks, but I felt it would be an uncivil thing to do, like withdrawing a present you'd made. And besides Estelle had stood up, too, and had her arms on my shoulders and seemed about to embrace me.

—I think of men like you as the wounded soldiers of this country, I have the healing touch.

Sure enough, she was embracing me now, her mouth was there right by my ear, her lips wet and hot like a buttered muffin, making me think I should eat a big steak for my dinner before returning to camp.

—This is a sad life, Walt, she whispered. There's nothing in it but to see young men go away, and what can a girl do?

—I'm sorry, kid, I said, trying to withdraw from her healing crush. You could go west, too, I added.

—Will you take me? she said, eagerly holding on to me and moving with my retreating steps so that by the time I could figure out an answer she had me pressed against the wall.

—You asked me that before, I said. You're doing good work here, with your healing touch and everything. America needs you right here.

—It's a poor life, she said, it gets me nowhere, you don't know what it's like not to have the freedom to spend a day out of these fancy clothes.

—Okay, so what do you want me to do, buy you some rags?

—You're without mercy, Walt, she said, withdrawing and returning to her chair. You do not know what a woman suffers in this world.

—Oh, come on sister.

—And my sister has to go without shoes in the winter. She's the sweetest little thing, Christine's her name but I call her Cindy, it's kind of cute, Cindy.

—Look, quit moaning, will you? Here's another ten bucks, buy her all the shoes you want.

I walked across the room and threw down a ten-dollar bill on the top of the fifty that I'd already put on the table, thinking to myself when I did that: Why're you doing this, Walt? All you've got to do is to walk out, you owe this woman nothing, come on, Walt, get the hell out, will you? Just then, as if she read my thoughts, she said, You owe me nothing! And had I been in my senses, I would undoubtedly have said, Sure, sister, you're damn right I owe you nothing, and I'd have picked up the sixty bucks and left. Instead, I said, Oh, come on, Estelle, a guy's got to help, it's nothing, I mean what's sixty lousy bucks, look, let me make it a neat hundred, it'll help you and everything, what's money to me, I'm going to be scooping up gold as soon as I hit California.

Sure, that's what I did, took out another forty bucks and put them right there on the table, it was a neat little pile, like I was playing a game of poker, or something. I've never been able to figure out what made me so crazy that night that I gave a hundred dollars to a girl I didn't even kiss.

—That's the way dames are, Josiah Clokey said when I told him the story when we were resting high up on the Rockies, he leaning against a rock on which many travellers had carved their names and beside which he had found Colonel Chenoweth's note.

—You're damn right, Dagger, I said, using Josiah Clokey's nick-name out of habit since we'd been together on the trail since leaving Fort Laramie.

—Yeah, Dagger said, the American dame has such a sharp tongue, she'll cut your heart in two and then nag the hell out of you for being so goddamn heartless. They're enough to make your cock recede into your belly. Which is why oral sex is such a hit in this country, there's nothing like it for drawing things out, and, what's more, it's like giving mouth-to-mouth aid to a guy who's almost drowned.

—You're no fool, Dagger.

—I've been around, he said, and I've seen the women try anything. It's a tough country for them. I've had my thrills, one way or another. And I don't expect to go to no heaven. That's a cheap salesman's trick. Mafia one at that.

—You're quite a philosopher, aren't you?

—I tell it like I see it, I told you I've been around, and believe me it's no use having fancy ideas when you don't know what you're talking about.

—Sure thing, Dagger, I said. But tell me something, Dagger. If you don't believe in anything, how do you expect me to pay any attention to what you say?

—Shit, you don't have to listen to me!

—It's good hearing you talk, though.

—That's none of my concern, okay?

—Sure, sure. But I do like to hear you talk, there's no one else out here. A man has to hear words.

—You should have brought that dame with you, Dagger said, she'd have given you an epic by the hour.

126

—She came, too, I said. There was a whole drama took place before you turned up. We were heading for the Little Blue River one day, all morning we could see the timberline on the bank of the river across the flat land. I loved the sun I was under, but I longed for the shade, too.

—It's some country, Dagger said.

—I figured we'd camp out there for a couple of days, let the horses and the oxen graze on what was left of the grass. There wasn't much, I could tell, not for miles on either side of the trail, there'd been so many emigrants before us. But I figured there'd be a bit more by the river, and, hell, it's good to rest by a river right in the middle of the goddamn country, we'd at least have water. Anyway, we came up to the river and there was another train already camped there. That was no surprise considering the traffic on the trail, besides the river was big enough for all of us, there was land for all of us. Sure, Dagger, there's land out there, in the prairie, for all of us and the Indians and the buffalo too, it's a great world out there, all we need is to work out a principle of sweet harmony. So, we camped there right next to this same Colonel Chenoweth's party of twenty wagons. There seemed to be a good many women in his party, but that was nothing irregular. It was only when it came to suppertime that we noticed that Colonel Chenoweth had only half a dozen male hands with him and that the rest of his party was entirely female, like he was in charge of an order of nuns or something. There were fifty or sixty of them, and what do you know, they'd all paid Colonel Chenoweth a hundred bucks each to take them west!

—Yeah, I know old Dick Chen, Dagger said, he ain't no Colonel o' nothin'. It's no surprise to learn that he escaped alone as he says on this note. He was born with ingenuity in his bones.

—Well, who should be among the women but Estelle! I couldn't believe it. I'd left her behind in Independence, and here she was ahead of me! I couldn't figure it out. Well, I thought, let bygones be bygones, a man needs a woman out here in the empty land, and thinking that it was my hundred dollars that was taking her west, I figured she owed me a lot more than just a pretty smile across from the fire where we sat eating buffalo burnt black with hickory smoke. Why, Estelle, I said to her after supper, it's a nice surprise meeting you here.

—Excuse me, she said, the name's Miriam.

—Oh, come on, I said, you're Estelle. I met you in the saloon in Independence where the English actor was walking crazily on the stage with a candle in his hand and screaming something about putting out the light when I left you, it seems just the other day, you were wearing a red chiffon dress and everything, and at first you called yourself Alice and gave me some bullshit about Santayana, remember? Those were the days, full of poetry, and that damned actor yelling about tomorrow and tomorrow and tomorrow like he'd forgotten the rest of the line.

—I don't know what you're talking about, Walt, she said.

—There you are! You know my name.

—Sure, I know your name, everyone does. You're leading that train, Colonel Chenoweth said so, There's this fella, Walt, he said, wants to camp with us and I guess it's okay with you ladies.

—Okay, Miriam, I said, I guess it makes no difference whether you're Estelle or Miriam, and I guess it makes no difference either if we never met before. It could have been something to talk about, that's all. But the past is the past, I guess.

—You have no sense of history, she said.

—Ha! Dagger let out a short, forced laugh.

—Sure, that's what she said, I said to Dagger. It's you, I said to her, who's denying her own history.

—You can't call that history, she said, what you've made up about me. It has no foundation in fact, is undocumented, and could be a symptom of lunacy. My past is my own, you know nothing about me.

—Okay, Estelle. Sorry, I mean Miriam, why don't we quit talking about the past?

—We never began talking about it, she said, we don't have a past. This is a young country, Walt.

We walked to the river and sat under a sycamore tree. It was nine in the evening but the sun hadn't touched the horizon yet. It was a cool, still evening.

—Ho, ho, cried Dagger. So what are you planning to tell me?

The sun set, the moon came up, sparkling wavelets danced on the water, and you lay there under the sycamore tree, your head now at Miriam's miraculous haloes, your hand now at the silk of her inner thighs, etfuckera, etfuckera, ho, ho!

—You're a poet, Dagger, but that's not what I was going to say. If it gives you a thrill, go ahead, let your imagination run wild, think of me as a great lover.

—I'm no poet, Dagger said, but I've never heard a guy talk of a woman without making her arms out to be marble and her thighs silk. I've heard a lot of shit in my time.

—Me too. But that's not what I was going to talk about.

—I wish you'd talk about it, Walt, Dagger said. It gives an old man a thrill to hear a little poetry. I don't mind a little fantasy. Marble and silk, ho, ho!

—Look, goddamnit let me finish what I have to say first, okay? There we were under the sycamore tree, Miriam and me. Sure, the sun set, the moon rose and the stars lit up, you know what it's like out there on the prairie, but all that was later. This was before the sun set, with the Little Blue River catching tones of red from the sky. Walt, Miriam says to me, whispering close to my ear, will you do something for me?

—Sure, honey, I said, I'd do anything for you.

—It's not a simple thing, she said, and maybe a girl should not be acting so bold if you know what I mean.

—Well, say what it is, I said, hoping she'd act real bold, and I'll tell you whether I can do it or not.

—Do you love me, Walt? she asked.

Now, what kind of a question is that? I wondered to myself. By her own account, I hadn't met her before in my life. When I did not answer for a couple of minutes, she said: Am I the kind of girl you like making love to?

Is that what she wants me to do to her, I wondered. But again I was lost for words, and looked to see how far the sun was from the horizon, another fifteen minutes maybe before the stars came out winking connivingly, I thought to myself, and heard her say: Walt, I want you to . . .

She stopped because I looked at her then, and she said,

speaking very softly, I'll make you a deal, I'll give you a hundred dollars for it.

Well, I thought, we're getting down to serious business now, we're being repaid the hundred bucks, the money's been on Estelle's conscience so much that she's changed her name. But I said: Look, honey, you don't need to pay me nothing, I'd love you for the way you are. You're swell, I added, giving a meaningful glance at her swellettes.

—Oh, Walt, she said, you're the sweetest soul I ever met! And she put her arms around me and gave me a tight hug and then said, You will be my savior, I know.

—What are you talking about, Miriam?

—Colonel Chenoweth is our escort to Sacramento, she said, but I know he's figuring to lose his way and have us stranded so that we'll end up owing him so much for food and shelter that we'd be obliged to work for him at you-know-what. I want you to help me escape from his train when we get to Fort Laramie. You can do it for love, and I mean real love, or for a hundred bucks, please yourself.

I was silent for a minute, for she'd asked me something far from what I'd expected. I'd thought she was about to say something like, Look, Walt, I know you're shy and everything and if it's a woman you want, you can have me, and I was fixing to reply, Why, Miriam, the thought hadn't occurred to me but now that you mention it it's a swell idea, what with the moon coming up and this gentle breeze from the Little Blue River, I sure am glad you thought of romance. And that's what I told her, kind of jokingly, hoping that she'd say, O well if that's what you want right now, okay, have me, but instead she said, Aw, shit, you guys have only one idea in your heads, how's a poor girl going to stand up for herself in this goddamn country? I told you, you can have me if you help me escape when we get to Fort Laramie.

—Ho, ho! Dagger laughed again. So you had to work for your bit of the slit, did you? You had to prove you were a man, ha, ha!

—It didn't happen that way, Dagger, I said. For when we were preparing to ford the Platte River, a horde of Pawnee warriors came down on us. We'd been told by some fur traders on their way to St Louis that it was a quiet summer for the white man because the Pawnee were at war with the Sioux and the Cheyennes, leaving the trail clear for the emigrants. But there they were just when we were figuring out how to take the wagons across the three-quarters of a mile of water with its bed of treacherous sand. You'd think that on the prairie you'd see a fly appear on the horizon fifteen miles away, but I swear we never saw the Pawnees until they were half a mile from us. The men in my train simply stood there gawping until the Pawnees were right on us. By the time we had sense enough to start firing, their arrows had struck deep into the hearts of a dozen of our men. But there was a great deal of firing going on and the Pawnees were falling from their horses like dead branches in a winter storm. Then I saw, far to my right, all the women in their long skirts, one knee on the ground, one eye shut, the head cocked back a little, rifles held against their shoulders, firing away and picking out the Pawnees like they were wooden ducks at a fair. Just when I was looking with astonishment at this incredible sight, two warriors rode up to me without my noticing them and stooping low on either side of me, they plunged their hands under my arms and, heaving me up, carried me away. I yelled and worked my legs as if I was running but I was a foot or two from the ground and was being carried by the two warriors on horses at such a pace that I went dizzy and soon passed out. Well, I was all that the Pawnees got from their raid, for when I came to I was in an Indian village and there was no sign of the white folks I'd been with on the banks of the Platte.

I was taken to a tepee where six braves sat in conference with a chief. Well, it was no conference really, for they weren't saying anything, just staring glumly at each other. There was smoke in the confined space and I thought for a moment maybe it's some kind of opium they've been puffing at that's put them in such a rarefied state of mind that they've freaked out. I was offered the distinction of sitting right in front of the chief whose name was never told me—it could have been something crazy like Old Hawk Eye or Chief Turkey Wattle, but the skin on his face and arms reminded me of cedar bark and that's how he exists in my mind, Chief Cedar Bark. He gave me a long thoughtful look with his bulging eyes, checking me over, and I stared right back at him from three feet away. He put a pipe to his mouth and took a couple of puffs, his eyes on me all the time. Then he held the pipe out to me, which I accepted with a smile and took a puff. Old Cedar Bark thrust his right hand before me and with a deft little gesture indicated I should smoke some more. I blew out enough smoke to create a cloud in front of me through which Cedar Bark appeared as some kind of genie, and returned the pipe.

—I'm sorry I don't have any gifts for you, I said. The circumstances of my coming here didn't give me the chance to do any shopping.

I said that to say something, to keep a hold over my mind, and not because I thought my words would have any meaning to the dumb freaks staring at me. I mean, I added for the same reason, it's a time-honored custom of our civilization to take gifts to one's hosts. We are people who prize courtesy as one of the higher virtues. Well, I spoke another sentence or two in the same vein and was warming up to a long speech of pretentious shit since there was nothing else to do; and so imagine my surprise when I saw Old Cedar Bark raise a hand and begin to address me in my own language.

—We know about your gifts, white man, he said. Bits of colored glass that you pass off as beads, little tin trumpets which your own children don't care to play with that you pass off as musical instruments, and as for the cheap home-made whiskey, that could be barley-water mixed with horse-piss for all I know.

—But your people have always enjoyed receiving them, I said.

—White man, when you receive a present from your brother and it's some cheap shoddy, worthless thing, do you ever throw it down with a look of great offense and proceed to abuse your brother, or do you not say, Thanks, Harry, that's just what I needed!

—Well, talking of whiskey, I said, I happen to have a flask in my pocket. I've been carrying it all the way from Kentucky in case of an emergency.

I took out the pint flask from my pocket and handed it to Cedar Bark with my compliments. He looked at it dubiously, uncorked it, sniffed, shook his head to suggest more doubt of its authenticity, tilted his head back and poured the pint of whiskey down his throat, swallowing it all in three gulps. He smacked his lips, hooded his eyes for a moment and shook his head, saying, Horse-piss!

I thought that I should have known better than to have thrown away good whiskey on someone who didn't appreciate it when I heard him say, But it comes from a pretty good horse!

—You can hold your liquor well, I said, being genuinely astonished that an old guy like him could swallow a pint of whiskey in three seconds and not be affected by it.

—I'm sorry I don't have any more, I said glancing at the six braves who still sat looking glum and with a resentful sort of admiration for their chief. We could have had a party, I added.

Old Cedar Bark made some high-pitched sounds, more a nasal whining than the expression of words, and the six braves rose, making ceremonious bows, and departed. The chief gave me a long stare, but there was no menace in his eyes, and I thought maybe the whiskey had had some effect after all. He picked up his pipe and sucked at it but finding that he could draw no smoke, expressed a moment's irritation with it and put it aside.

—Well, he said, what would you like to ask me?

—I beg your pardon? I said.

—I believe you heard my words, he said. There is no storm here, no wind to carry away the words, no thunder or the creaking or crackling of trees, in fact if I spoke at a much lower volume, ninety per cent lower say, you'd still hear me without any trouble.

—Excuse me, I said, I heard the words but it was your meaning that escaped me.

—Why didn't you say so instead of pretending you hadn't heard me? If you're not going to use words correctly, then we might as well use sign language, at least with that one never knows how absurdly one has been misunderstood. But deception is second nature to you, you can think only in terms of taking advantage through subtle deceptions, you'll perpetrate any treachery.

—Now there you're using words in a way that I don't understand.

—A hypocritical pretense to innocence also comes naturally to you, he said.

133

—Excuse me once again, I said. But please tell me first what crime I've committed.

—None has been reported, he said. Why should you jump to such absurd conclusions? We're talking of abstract matters which are more important than your obsessive concern with yourself. The only question that should interest you right now is what you're doing here. Instead, you just sit there quite complacently with not a care in the world.

—Okay, tell me what am I doing here?

—How should I know! I have no insight into the processes of your mind.

—Why was I brought here, then?

—Ah, that is a different question altogether.

—Well, do you have an answer to it? I asked.

—I could give you several answers, he said. What would you say if I said that you were chosen as an excellent example of your race so that the scientists of our tribe could study your behavior to prove certain conclusions that they've already formulated but are anxious to have proved? Or, I could answer you by saying that you were brought here to be questioned about the intentions of the white man in this land of ours so that our warriors could then devise a plan of attack. Or, I could say that we intend to cut your throat in order to give ourselves the satisfaction of symbolically punishing your race. But of course I'm not going to suggest any of these because you're not going to think them credible since you're not prepared to credit me or my tribe with the kind of rationalization any one of these answers entails, for you will believe only your own preconceptions—which no doubt inform you that we're a bunch of wild savages, naïve, innocent and barbaric.

—I don't understand you, I said.

—That doesn't surprise me in the least. For a start, you expected nothing but coarse grunts from me and some dramatic gestures. Maybe I'd pass some cruel judgement, you no doubt thought, and it would be the end of your days except that the U.S. cavalry, bugles blowing and the stars and stripes rippling against the blue sky, would come to your rescue at the last minute, we would all be wiped out and you'd be left alone in the middle of the village embracing the high-bosomed, blue-eyed girl from Kentucky. Your imagination expects only the expected. All your beliefs are fantastic.

—Can I ask again why I was brought here?

—There you go again with your petty obsession with yourself! Let me tell you something, Walt.

—How do you know my name?

—Is that really your name?

—Sure, why else should you have called me Walt just now?

—Oh, for a most improbable reason. The first white man I ever met was called Walt and since then I've tended to think of all white men as Walt. Had he been George, I'd have called you George. What should it matter? If you don't believe this story, then attribute my naming you correctly to pure coincidence. That's life, things happen for no reason. But it's interesting, is it not, this attachment you have to your name, as if it were some guarantee of immortality? However, to come to your question which frankly bores the ass off me: our warriors lost badly today though I hear it was your women who saved you and that the men among you proved to be cowards. Be that as it may, our men lost, but to save something of their reputation among their own women, who are great artists at mockery and derision, they brought you here and so proved their heroism. I see from your look that you do not believe me. Well, let me say this. There was born to our tribe a great princess many years ago. At that time we were at war with some of your fur-traders who had at first, as usual, come to us with beads, toy trumpets etbitera, but let's not start that again. Our elders and priests at that time decided, having seen God knows what portents, that the baby princess should be put in a basket and left to float upon the river so that she would be out of danger. Well, she has never been found since and our priests, always coming up with more and more damnable portents to appease our womenfolk, who have an incredible appetite for drama, have come up with the notion that a white man is destined to find her and to restore her to the tribe. To tell you the truth, I don't mind this kind of superstition, for it relieves me of all responsibility: if she's found, I can always claim how just and god-fearing I was in listening to the priests, and if she's not, I can always blame the white man for being totally unreliable and untrustworthy. So, there you have your answer, you're the white man chosen for this wonderful task, and whether or not you succeed at least you'll have a great story to tell your kids.

—Where should I go to look for her? I asked.

—You come from east of the Missouri and are going west of the Rockies. He who travels the entire country will see her— that's one of our priests' idiotic sayings, they're always dreaming up proverbial-sounding phrases to impress the women.

—What kind of a person am I to look for? I mean is there any description of the princess I can go by?

—None of us has seen her since she was a baby.

—So, how will I know her when I see her?

—She will be the most beautiful thing you ever saw.

—What kind of language is that?

—Cryptic and meaningless, I agree. I fear that's the way our priests talk and I can't be more helpful than that.

—It might take me all my life and I still might not find her.

—We're a patient people, Old Cedar Bark said.

—We measure time, I said, by the effectiveness of our actions, output and growth against hours and days.

—Please don't tell me about that, it means nothing to me, and besides it's your problem. I don't have to start on metaphysics which will tell us nothing after we've exhilarated ourselves with pompous thoughts. I know everything and I am bored.

—Well, when do I start my search for the princess? I asked.

—When you leave here, tomorrow, or the day after. We've got a feast for you tonight, another asinine prescription of our damned priests.

—When I asked you where I should go in search of her, you gave me a vague answer.

—I can't be more helpful than that. These are profound matters.

—But if I spent my entire lifetime looking for her and did not find her, how would you ever now that I'd indeed spent my time in the search and not, for example, passed the rest of my days in drunkenness and debauchery?

—You will always be looking for her whatever you do, that is the burden you must live with from now, in fact you will live it from now on, for you have no choice. But as you can observe, this kind of talk makes me uncomfortable; I have an abhorrence for obfuscation, however politically necessary it might be to talk in riddles. You have your burden, what else do you want in life? We'd better go and join the feasting. There is to be food, singing and dancing, and the priests, in their imbecilic concern for rituals of their own devising, have picked out a virgin for you to spend the night with, it's supposed to be a sacrifice.

—Ho, ho, Dagger cried aloud. You old rogue, it had to come to that sooner or later, ho, ho. Frippery and froppery, trout, salmon and sturgeon, Walt's balls are coppery as he fucks the Indian virgin!

—Oh, come on, Dagger, that's not the truth, you know that. And I know your idea of an Indian virgin is of some slim-waisted slippery creature with a flawless complexion and bright eyes, her straight black hair combed neatly down with a middle parting, secured by a headband that comes across the forehead and has a couple of feathers tucked in at the back, to say nothing of the satiny dress with its two revelations.

—That's what I like, Dagger said, poetry.

—But the lady who entered my tepee that night was preceded by a foul smell and when she appeared she seemed to be five feet tall and three feet wide, with great globes for cheeks and eyes sunk way back a couple of feet, no neck at all, and her wiry hair was speckled with lice. If there was a virgin about to be attacked, it was yours truly. It was some sacrifice. I don't even want to talk about it. It was the greatest trial I've had to endure in my life.

—You see, Dagger, I figured out later that Old Cedar Bark sending me out to go in search of the lost princess was simply finding a shrewd way to let me go from his tribe. He reckoned his warriors had made a mistake capturing me, it would only attract more trouble from the white man. But he couldn't let me loose, it would be politically unwise for it would appear to be an insult to the warriors, so he worked out a way I could do a great favor to the tribe by leaving it. But I don't mind admitting to you, Dagger, that even when I'm out in the empty land I keep looking, like Old Cedar Bark told me, for the most beautiful thing I ever saw. As he said, I have no choice.

So, I rode alone to Fort Laramie, glad again to be one of a confusion of humanity. My companions had already gone, and I did not begrudge them their haste, knowing how anxious they were to see their eyes reflected in the gold of California, but Colonel Chenoweth's party was still there. Apparently, the ladies were a rare feast for the eyes of the soldiers and the traders at the fort, and had been begged to stay longer, the traders' entreaties having been accompanied by presents of fur which it would have been cruel to refuse. A carnival atmosphere prevailed, with singing and dancing every night and huge feasts of venison and buffalo meat. The first time I saw Miriam, she was walking across the courtyard of the fort, her hand at the sleeve of a young soldier. I did not speak to her until I found her alone in the evening in-between dances.

—Why, hi, there, Walt, she said, did the Pawnees mate you with all their women?

—Oh, come on Miriam, what kind of talk is that?

—Just teasing you, she said, laughing. But seriously, we were thinking of coming to your rescue.

—Well, I've come to rescue you.

—I'm doing fine, she said.

—But you said that night by the Little Blue River that you wanted to be rescued from Colonel Chenoweth.

—It was nice by the river, she said, the moon coming up and everything, guess it made me feel romantic.

—Not at all, you had no romantic ideas at all. Instead, you made me promise . . .

—Look, Walt, I'm having a great time here, and if you'll excuse me, I promised the next dance to my pretty Sergeant.

—So that's what it is.

—Sure, a girl has to keep hoping, there are too many disappointments in this life.

—Okay, please yourself, it's your life.

But late that night a scout rode into the fort with news of some fur-traders up river being ambushed by a party of Sioux and by early morning Miriam's blue-eyed soldier had ridden out with his company. In the afternoon, Colonel Chenoweth announced that he was planning to resume his trek west the next day and ordered the ladies to be prepared and in their wagons by four in the morning. Miriam came to me after dinner that night.

—It'll have to be tonight, she said.

—What's that? I asked.

—That you must take me away. And I will keep my part of the promise.

—Yesterday you as good as told me to quit the universe.

—I was just testing you, to see if you'd get jealous. Walt, I don't mind telling you I'm proud of you. I need you to save me. You've seen for yourself how Colonel Chenoweth's been treating us, throwing us at the lecherous soldiers. You can't imagine what will happen to us when we get to California.

—Thanks for your faith in me, lady, but I don't mind telling you that I think you're mad. You'll say anything, do anything, to get a bit of drama out of life. You don't exactly tell lies, but your fantasies are out of this world.

Dagger had gone to sleep, leaning against the rock, so I quit talking to him. I felt restless, I wanted to get up and move on. It had been a long, difficult journey so far but when I looked back on it, I enjoyed remembering the most troublesome times, those which needed resources of strength, courage and patience that none of us thought we had: getting the wagons down steep banks and into rivers of shifting sand, hauling them up again, having to unload them and putting the supplies on the backs of mules and, once across, re-loading the wagons. Sometimes half a day would be lost crossing a stream not twenty yards wide. There were days when it rained so persistently it was better not to travel rather than risk chafing the horses and the oxen where the wet harness rubbed their skin. Except when it rained, we rose early, never later than four o'clock, in order to overtake other trains which still slept so that we would find some grass left for our animals, and when the others began to catch on to this trick we found ourselves waking at two in the morning until this competition for good grass became so ridiculous that we reverted to rising at four. We had raw bacon for our supper, and once a week a glorious feast of bean soup. There was game on the land, we often sighted antelope and white-tailed deer, and sometimes a couple of us would go after them, but too often we were determined to move on and were prepared to forego fresh meat for an extra mile. We would sacrifice anything that could remotely be construed to be pleasure for the sake of territorial advantage; success was the only important thing and the very act of being on the move was sufficient to give us a keen sense of achievement. And there were the buffalo, of course, herds of several thousand out on the horizon, their rumbling being carried across the empty land hours before they came to view. The country gave me other visions, other dreams that I still carry within my breast after so much that has happened.

At Fort Laramie, I decided not to join Colonel Chenoweth's train of lunatic women and planned to continue on my own. On the night before I was to leave, I was coming out of a dry-goods store when I ran into Dagger. He was an odd sight, for he was dressed in a buff vest which had all its buttons missing, knee breeches which perhaps lived up to their name by having holes where all the world could see that their owner possessed a pair of healthy knees, and on his shoes were silver buckles that had long been tarnished. He had a great deal of dirty hair on his head that he'd tied in a queue. He had obviously once been a gentleman. We got talking and since he was planning to ride out west the next day, too, we decided to journey together.

He came from Boston, he told me as we rode out in the morning. He had walked all the way to Fort Laramie two years ago and then gone north to join the fur trappers. He had made money, good money, he said, but had gambled it all away. It's not the money, he said, chuckling to himself, hell, I could have made a fortune staying in Boston. And it wasn't for the lack of money that I walked two thousand miles. Truth is, I was in no hurry, I never had any anxiety for anything. I just wanted to take it slow and cool, one step at a time right across the country. I just wanted to move slow enough so that I could see everything about me. If

I made a fortune in one place, then I'd have to stay there. So, I prefer to fail every time I'm near to making it. I don't choose to fail, it just happens every time that I fail, and after it's happened, I'm glad it has and say to myself that's how I want it, to fail so that I don't get stuck with success, and that's how I prefer it if I really thought of making a choice. Luckily, there's always women and gamblers waiting to take your money from you, it's a great thrill to throw your money away enjoying yourself. And the greatest thrill is to wake up after a night of debauchery to discover that you've lost everything, that you've once again recovered the freedom to be alone and out on the road. You know what makes me happy? Looking about me when I'm out like this, looking at the big world and saying to myself, there it is, the big world. There it is, Walt, there it is. And he flung his arms to indicate the circle of the horizon around us.

The land we traversed was covered with artemisia, that bitter shrub whose pre-eminence argued the sterility of the land, for the wild sage grew in a land that had surrendered its soil to wind, ice and rain.

—There's this to the land, too, Dagger said, an uncompromising reluctance to live up to man's expectations. It will turn its hard back on you, the son of a bitch, remind you of finalities when you're only interested in looking for somewhere to start a family.

But the next day we were among pines and cottonwoods, entering forests that were both fearful and enchanting, for here were the dark gorges, narrow gullies, and here the canyons, waterfalls and bouncing streams. Here was the silence of tall trees and the laughter of water. Here were rocks that thrust themselves above the lowly vegetation, sheer polished surfaces of granite. The country here was so magnificent in its variety and scale, so outrageously arrogant in its self-definition, its steep and seemingly bottomless descents and its upward wall-like thrustings, that Dagger said aloud, Is it I who witness all this? The sky above us was blue and the peaks of the Rockies that we had begun to recognize from the notes of previous travellers were white with snow. Little blue and violet flowers grew in our path, and lichen spreading its velvet fur across the lower rocks mixed browns, yellows and russet hues in its preponderant green. Is it I? Dagger muttered again, chuckling to himself, greatly bemused.

We climbed above a pine forest and rode across something of a plateau where we decided to rest before following a trail down into a valley that was a small pass through the mountain range. Leaving the horses to graze, we sat beside a rock, at first examining the various signatures former travellers had left upon the rock. None of the names was familiar but it was comforting to know that we were not alone in this world, that others had pursued the same journey and had somehow endured its trials. I saw a piece of paper at the foot of the rock, a large stone upon it to keep it from being carried away by the wind, and picked it up. The writing on it had not been disfigured by rain or the passage of time, and I thought to myself that whoever put it there must have been pretty sure that there were travellers hard on his heels for otherwise it was a waste of time leaving ink on paper out on the top of a plateau. I looked at the signature. It was that of Colonel Chenoweth. The note was brief: Ambushed by Crow. Men killed. Women abducted. Horses and wagons stolen. In their mercy, Crow gave me a lame mule on which I proceed to California through the shorter desert route.

Dagger and I talked of what we could do. Nothing really, we concluded, for the two of us could not take on the might of the Crow. So we sat there chewing some jerked buffalo meat, talking idly, watching our horses at their meal in the distance. I told various stories of my experiences, making them as interesting as I could, adding a little colorful embroidery here and there, but, absorbed in my own inventive narrative, I didn't notice that rather than amuse old Dagger, I'd merely put him to sleep, for there he sat, leaning against the rock, his head fallen forward on his chest.

—What I know of Miriam, I was saying, I guess she'll be all right, she'll get the drama she's so damn crazy about, and I guess she'll make out fine with a young Crow warrior. Why, it wouldn't surprise me if she so works things out that she'll have the entire Crow nation at her mercy.

I decided to say no more since it was obvious that Dagger had ceased to hear me and I was uttering any old nonsense anyway. I was just about to rise and go attend to the horses, but just before I lifted myself up, I looked at Dagger in an indulgent sort of way, and was half up from the ground and was just about to make some joke to see if he was fully asleep or not, when I saw that when I had observed his head fallen on his chest earlier I had not then seen, for I did not expect to see any such thing, an arrow stuck to his bosom, the blood pouring out, and the simple fact that my friend Dagger was no longer alive.

I wasted no time attending to poor Dagger's body, providing him with as comfortable a resting place as I could devise with the tools at my disposal and finding a flat rock to serve as his headstone upon which I inscribed his name together with the words GENTLEMAN FROM BOSTON, and then finding that I had crowded the words at the top of the stone, leaving so much blank space that the layout looked inelegant, I added in big letters: HE LAUGHED AND LAUGHED.

All the while that I worked on the grave and the headstone, I asked myself again and again why was it that the Indians had picked out only Dagger and why had they not simultaneously, or a moment later, or even a moment earlier, shot an arrow into my breast, too. Why had they chosen to kill only one of us, and having done so, why had they chosen Dagger and not me? What had they decided was to be my destiny? And surely, they could not have gone away after killing only one of us. They were there, somewhere behind the trees or the bushes or the rocks, had been there for the last two hours while I buried Dagger and scraped away at the gravestone; they had had ample opportunity to kill me but had not done so. And if they wanted to capture me alive, that too could easily have been accomplished by now. That they had done nothing but only filled me with the horrors of the possibilities of what they might do was what scared me. And what scared me even more was that they might do nothing at all, simply leave me alone so that my mind would persuade me that, like Colonel Chenoweth, I should attempt the shorter route to California, through the desert.

VIII

Terminal Scripts

Call from H.: Saw subject in a black '39 Buick, stopped at toll-booth, headed for Oakland. Coat collar turned up, hat pulled down. Driver a woman of twenty-six to twenty-eight, dark hair, recently permed, green tigerish eyes, orange blouse with long pointed collar. Subject obviously hitched a ride. Woman appeared to laugh light-heartedly, cannot be aware of danger to herself. There are certain moral questions here that I'd like to discuss with you sometime. And other complex matters. E.g., why in a context of interminable motion are conclusions necessary? Second, why a sensation is unforgettable. Third, why cannot words function without interpretation which necessarily involves chimeras? Fourth, what about unintentional lies? Fifth, what about false convictions? Sixth ...

—Sure, sure, I broke in before his ellipse landed him on the moon, and asked for the license plate number. What's that, I shouted, IOWA?

—Yes, he said calmly, it's an Iowa plate, which is hardly surprising since people from all over the country visit San Francisco and have their stereotyped expectations fulfilled by what in truth is a vulgar and a barbaric city.

—Spare me that, brother, I said, and he: Certainly, my dear fellow, it's Iowa all right, nothing extraordinary about that in itself. It could as easily have been Florida or Maine.

—Okay, okay, I screamed back, spare me the speculations, brother, just spill out the damn facts.

—Did you not yourself come this way? he asked. I seem to recall your story.

—Shit, yes! I cried aloud, But this is not a time for nostalgia.

—I understand that perfectly, he said, this is a forward looking nation.

—O Christ, I don't mean that, I said, I'd be the last one to forget my history, but what can you say about words put together?

—Even after a careful analysis of journals, diaries, public records, letters, newspaper accounts, messages scratched upon rocks?

—Sure, I said, words that interpret words, they form only a vocabulary for the living and what happens can only be seen to happen, who can tell?

—You put it admirably, he said, and if it's not too tedious a joke, I might almost say you take the words out of my mouth. And that's been the problem, having to recollect and re-arrange the images while observing what's going on, one had to live three separate lives simultaneously.

—I'd say you've a whole lot more than three lives, brother, seeing you I'd say you're a whole family of cats in one.

—As for the lady in the black Buick, he said, I do not believe she will come to any harm.

—I suppose she has the car radio on, though, I said. That'll be a moment!

—Very likely, he said, the news should be on in another minute, on the half-hour, and I suppose you've already put out a description.

—Sure, sure, I said, the entire country knows the shape and texture of his hat, to say nothing of that sad, cynical, bitter voice. But I don't guess she's going to be frightened, more likely she'll fall in love with him, these things have a way of confounding the expected, all our projections and predictions can lie back on the couch of laboratory logic, there's no saying what the hell a dame driving out of San Francisco is likely to do.

—Certainly, the element of caprice cannot be accounted for in advance, he said.

—Nor stupidity, brother, nor the human incapacity to act rationally in dangerous situations, nor plain female contrariness, and nor the sudden desire to succumb to the thrill of danger, just for the hell of it, a moment's whim is all you need for your science to fall on its ass.

—Of course, he said, if he, too, were to fall in love with her,

145

it would create problems: she would reform his character, but, alas, at what cost? Only to lose him, and were she to accept his dominance and accede to his way of life, she would lose herself. A tragic outcome seems certain, though I'd be the last to predict one.

—Drama, whatever happens, I said. One event upon another.

—Yes, drama, he said, there's no escaping what the people want. And that's what keeps one alert to improbability, those surprises by which we can still be surprised, the extraordinary shape of things.

—Only things? I asked.

—No, he answered, I was talking of the shape of things and not of things which have a shape.

—I see, I said. I don't know a butterfly but I can see the shape of a butterfly.

—You are most resourceful, he said, most felicitous in your choice of example, the observation could not have been more precise.

—And nor, I said, could it have been, in a manner of speaking, more meaningless.

—Absolutely, he said, and what is more, meaningless to the highest degree of intellectual satisfaction, for what greater understanding can we want?

—So, we proceed through negations, is that it?

—Sir, we proceed, he said. That is all our vanity demands.

—Look, I said, the guy could pull a gun on her, what then?

—I presume, he said, by now you have called in all units, and got the highway patrol to set up road-blocks.

—Sure, they're burning up gas and rubber all over California, I said, but what kind of a drama is it to be, for god's sake? I mean the D.A. is screaming shit right up my ass.

—I can understand that, he said. A lawyer has his problems, it's no use listening to him, archaic vengeance has no place here. As for our man pulling a gun on the lady, I believe that's not quite in character, and in such a matter one would not wish to offend the nation's taste.

—Okay, so we've got a goddamn lunatic, I said.

—Well, I would not go as far as that, he said. Passion supposedly observes propriety, and your criminals are depicted to be good

146

chaps at heart.

—Yeah, I said, they're the ones considered romantic. A man on the run is a hero because he's running while we're all selling insurance or real estate in Omaha, Nebraska, or Louisville, Kentucky. It's thrilling to observe the nonconformists, it's an American pastime, there's an unexpressed admiration for the gangster.

—Movement, flight, the ability to appear with astonishing speed at unexpected places, these, too, he said.

—Sure, I said, I've seen Indians on ponies chase the buffalo, I've seen them on canoes riding rapids of more turbulence than a plane meets in a hurricane.

—I say, he said, you have been around.

—I've seen a few things, I said, and I've a photographic memory for details, it's part of the training, I don't forget any shit. Say, did I ever tell you what happened to Miriam?

—Is that relevant? he asked.

—Sure, brother, it's as relevant as the smog you're breathing.

—Then please spare me a narrative of it, he said, for I'd rather not know, at least it's not what I want to know, what I'm trying to establish.

—Hey, what shit is this? I yelled. Who's being all snootily privately exclusively uppity-da?

Just when I said that, I saw something that made me laugh uproariously.

—What are you laughing about? he asked.

—I just heard this black pimp go up to a German tourist walking down Forty-second street and say, Hi there, Fritz, would you like a pair o' tits? How's that for sheer brass, hey, brother?

—Well, that's hardly to the point, he said, and besides I thought you were in your office in L.A.

—That is precisely the point, brother, if you'll give it your kind consideration.

—I say!

—Say nothing, brother, there's no harm done.

—I do see your point, however, he said.

—I'm touched by your humility, I said.

—My mind puzzles over that, he said, disregarding my irony, the notion of simultaneity, it's difficult, but time and space, yes, decidedly it's difficult, though of course one must never neglect common day-to-day etcetera.

—Will you establish norms? I asked. Absolutes?

—No, no, of course not.

—Well, what's this shit about common experience, then?

—I did say I was puzzled.

—Casuistry, brother, it's all casuistry.

—Now there you are offering an absolute, he said triumphantly.

—You should meet some poets while you're out there, I said, there's a whole bunch of them, they think living in San Francisco is a guarantee of authenticity.

—I have listened to them, he said, and I did observe this curious syllogism: I make utterances, I live in San Francisco, therefore, I am a poet.

—Yeah, they think they're the real thing, I said, and perhaps some are, who knows?

—Indeed, he said, though I should want more meaning before agreeing that words are only words. Whereas canvas and color, sounds in the air, forms of steel, wood or stone, other dimensions altogether, chimeras that fulfil an eye or an ear that would perceive, being accustomed to the habits of the tribe.

—You're a visionary, brother, you know where the oases are.

—No, no, I'm as hard as flint and my grunting is as guttural and unharmonious as a stone-age man's.

—Sure, you have my sympathy, brother, you should come down to L.A., I'll take you around Hollywood, and there's a whole bunch of files right here on my desk for you to check through. They'll tickle your ass, at least, if not your fancy.

—Too many of them end in a blood-bath, he said, others come to implausible conclusions.

—Oh, come on now, brother, what goes on for real in this state is incredible.

—I know, I know, he said, but I was thinking for example of his flying from Alaska to Washington, D.C., non-stop some forty years ago, using additional exterior detachable fuel-tanks which he discards to reduce the weight while flying on the regular tanks and still runs out of fuel within twenty miles of the capital and then miraculously glides in to make a perfect landing.

—It's all here, I said.

—To say nothing of narrow escapes from a French penal colony or a German occupied town, he said, or survival against all odds in a raft in the north Atlantic or in the Sierra Madre or coming out unmarked from a hail of machine-gun fire.

—Oh, a little fantasy hurt no one, I said, they're the velvet stuff of popular dreams, for the truth is that something endures in spite of the imbecility of conception, the question is what and why, after you've taken away the folksy events, just as a squirrel jumping from one tree to another and disappearing among its branches still leaves its arc in the air, essences, brother, essences, you still see the arched tail following the parabolic leap of the body, and long after you see neither the body nor the tail the arc still persists.

—But what remains, he asked, if what you've seen is a man in a white dinner jacket, drink in hand, eyes sad, listening to another singing a song at the piano? Surely, not his trite romanticism? You see, what appear to be clues only add to the mystery.

—Good thing, too, brother, it keeps us in business.

—You must grant me, then, that the sun rising and setting keeps Time in business.

—Oh, sure, I said, why not? I knew a guy in St Louis who'd bring a rocking chair out to the front porch the moment the sun rose and sit rocking there all day long and then at sunset he'd stand up, stretch himself, and saying, There goes another goddamn day, pick up the chair and withdraw to the house. He lived to be eighty-three.

—My earlier question was, What remains?

—Well, as I was saying, there's a whole bunch of files on my desk, there are some facts which might make more sense to you, you know how it is, a fresh eye will see things you don't, or a mind trained differently will turn obvious facts into phenomena of extraordinary meaning.

—I shall be glad to look into anything that comes my way, he said, but that's not what I meant.

—I know what you mean, I said, have no fear, friend, I understand you to the nicest implication. The only thing I don't understand in this life is math. Talk of Xs and Ys and put them together with a lot of piggly-wiggly symbols and my mind goes blank, unless you tell me the X stands for something else, even a damn number, I'm lost, the idea of X being X and NOTHING ELSE is beyond me, brother, I mean what the hell does that mean? And musical notation, that's just murder. The other day I saw a guy at the airport, sitting reading a book and shaking his head as if he was at the Symphony. I walked past behind him and saw that it wasn't a novel or something but some musical score he had in front of him. A guy's got to be crazy to look at a page full of black marks and hear music. I mean with not even a pocket transistor plugged into his ear. Sensational, what mankind manages to do one way or another, a lot of it supported by theory, belief and fanaticism.

—That's simple enough, he said, some people have a gift for foreign languages, for example.

—You know when I was in Italy during the war, I said, not knowing any Italian, whenever I talked to the natives I spoke English with an Italian accent. Excuse-a me, I kept saying to everyone, even to the whore who tried to pick me up in Naples, Excuse-a me, I said, I donna think you're-a worth-a ten dahlers. She called me a son of a beach, and I said, That's-a okay, sister. Believe me, friend, we're a courteous people when we're abroad.

What was that he said? Roy Earle, Big Shot Earle they called him, you were just rushing toward death, he said. It was a sad part, even a criminal can be a tragic hero, and the girl who would not leave her dog behind, it was really sad. You could never mean nothing to me. Nothing special that is. If you get what I mean. I knew why he said that but the girl didn't and she wouldn't leave him and had to come back to him with the dog in a basket. The bit about the dog made him wild. Mad dog Earle, how do you like that? But he said it without being mad at the dog, in a way that conveyed affection for the dog. He had the country crying, believe me. There was the crowd of cops, reporters and spectators on the side of the mountain with him high up there among the boulders, and cops calling to him to come down, and one cop got near him and he fired a whole lot of shot at him while calling to the cop, Come and get me, buddy, come and get me. What's the matter cop, yeller? But the dog came out of the basket, looked at the feet around him with his innocent round eyes, and a cop saw the dog which ran up the mountain straight for Earle. That was it. It was inevitable. From the start, there was no way the dog's innocence wasn't going to be instrumental in the final tragedy. That's what you say, copper. But they got him all right. Big Shot Earle, look at him lying there, he's not much is he? But the girl asks, Mister, what does it mean when a man crashes out? Liberty, sister, freedom, independence, love, tenderness, life, existence, reality. You can't take it away, you can't take it.

Just when I put the phone down, the door was flung open dramatically and Rosemary walked in, exaggeratedly mimicking the swinging gait of a fashion model. She wore a dark green summer dress with white polka-dots, cut in a V at the neck where two rows of white pearls together shaped a quarter moon, a white, wide-brimmed hat on her head, white gloves and shoes and handbag. She took off her sun-glasses, screwed up her eyes for a moment against the glare from the window and said, Hi there, Walt, thought I'd bring a breath of ecstasy to your sweaty, stinking, lousy world.

She walked right up to me, held my face, the handbag dangling from one hand and falling against my shoulder, gave me a distant kiss that had the effect only of blowing perfumed warmth at my mouth, and sat back on the edge of the desk with one foot on my chair.

—What are you trying to do, Rosemary, dispense erections to the police force?

—In this city? You're joking! The way I'm dressed no man looks at me.

—Oh, come on.

—Sure! Wearing a dress in L.A. is like being in purdah, no one looks at you unless you've something on display. I was lunching with a movie director, that hot turd Jackie Gross, and he could have been an Arab sitting with his mother in Beirut. Oh, let me tell you what happened. Bemice Bauer walked up to our table during coffee, well she didn't exactly walk up, snaked up perhaps, or hipped to the left while titting to the right, and having to pass through the narrow gap between two chairs she turned sideways and raised a ballooning bottom, well she came right up to us in her dress of silver threads that had been woven like a Yucatan hammock. Christ, EVERYTHING was on display, rocking away in that goddamn hammock! She was standing right beside me, her waist at the level of my eyes, and what do you know, Walt, her rockettes weren't the only thing free behind those silver chains, shit, she had nothing on underneath, NOTHING, Jesus, I could even see her publicity hairs which were red, too, like her head, she must rinse them with the same shampoo with the extra strong tint. Mah fayvrut directah! she cried with the enthusiasm of a queen for her husband's treasurer, grasping Jackie Gross's tiny little head with its hair of grey wire-wool to her bosom and pressing her left freedom fighter to his cheek. Whu-y, honey, she drawled, baby Bemice has juss bin dyin' to kees your burnin' brow. I don't know what brow she was talking of, for she went ahead and kissed Jackie right on the mouth, all passionate, like he was Robert Redford or somebody. Wiell, honey, she said, ah guess ah'11 have to wait for more, so you don't forgayt to call, remember baby Bernice loves you. And she rocked, wiggled, undulated and snaked right out of sight. And you know that miserable son of a bitch didn't even bat his weary eye-lids, just picked up his cup of coffee, took a sip and said, They don't write scripts like they used to, an agent called me a week ago and said, Jackie I've a hot script here, it'll knock .... Okay, okay, I said, cut out the superlatives, just tell me what it is, and he said C'mon, bud, this is your pal Rudi, Sure, I said, sure Rudi, just give it to me plain will you, I haven't the time for the garnish. Okay, he said, you're the boss, well it's about Indians, but just wait till you hear the details, there's a tribe of Indians who've been living peacefully on their reservation for a hundred years, unmolested by the white man etcetera, doing their pottery and weaving etcetera, putting up with the usual tourists through their pueblo, but unknown to the tourists or the U.S. marshals or the federal government etcetera, they've a vast underground laboratory where their scientists have been perfecting a new bomb, well, bud, this takes up half the movie, gradually begins to suggest the potential horror for by now it's hinted they plan to take over the U.S.A. The rest follows from there, how they train their secret army, and there are shots of the good old white folks living in their good old black and white towns innocently going about playing football, selling insurance, and generally working their asses off to keep America a great democracy etcetera while the Indians are ruthlessly going about their plan to wreck the country. And then there's a great climax, bombers heading for the White House, the Capitol and the Empire State Building, the great panic in the Pentagon, the President on the phone to the Indian chief, and then the great resolution, who do you think saves the situation? It's fantastic, you'll never believe it! A girl, an Indian girl who'd earlier fallen in love with a white tourist and gives him, at the last anguished moment, the secret which would divert the Indian bombers, Jesus, Jackie, you'll have the whole country crying at the end of the movie. Look, Rudi, I said, call me back another time, will you, when you have a script a guy can work with? Well, what do you know, old Ron Renfrew bought that for fifty grand and has already raised twenty million to make it!

—Rosemary, I said, I appreciate all this gossip but I have work to do.

—You call it gossip? Rosemary asked in her ringing voice. Understand, Walt, I bring you news from the principal artery that comes out of the heart of western civilization. What kind of a kick do you think a girl gets watching the mauve and pink webbing on Jackie Gross's weary eye-lids for three hours? Bosomy Bernice might hope for a part, but I've nothing to gain from the guy. Listening to his weary commentary on the excellence of food, which, believe me, was lousy, or his evil pronunciation of French when he orders wine he doesn't understand is enough work for me, and thank God I don't have to fling opportune titties his way. And a lot of thanks I get for my hard work, gossip he calls it!

—I'll remember it, I said, I'll put it to good use, don't you worry, Rosie.

—Well, do me the favor then and listen. There's a script Jackie is interested in buying, it's a revenge theme with the most elaborate murder you can think of. It's set in a fashionable part of San Francisco in the magnificent mansion of the Risvold family. Paul Risvold, forty-two, married to the glamorous Louise, with two children, is the most discriminating and distinguished art collector. It's a wonderful, beautiful world that he's put together in his mansion, people fly in from New York to his parties. But way back when he was starting and was a comparative pauper, he was travelling in Europe with his friend George. Paul's interest at that time was only in girls whereas the brilliant George cared only for art objects which he lusted after. Well, the two are in some broken down junk shop in Clapham, London, and come across an old painting. George realizes it's a long lost Rembrandt and finding that he doesn't have on him the ten pounds the man wants for the tarnished old frame around the picture asks Paul to lend him the money. Paul looks at his wallet and says he doesn't have any since he forgot to cash his travellers' checks. The two catch a bus back to their hotel in South Kensington so that George can get the ten pounds he has hidden in a sock, telling the shopkeeper they'd be back for the picture. Just before the bus reaches the river, Paul says there's no need for him to go to the hotel and return to Clapham and he'd rather spend the afternoon at the Battersea Fun Fair and so he gets off the bus. As soon as the bus is over the river, Paul hails a taxi, drives back to the shop, tells the man there that he's back for the picture, buys it for ten pounds, tells the man that if his friend returns to buy the picture to tell him that a German tourist had bought it, explaining that he wants to surprise his friend, etcetera. Well, that's the background to Paul's present success. He'd hid the Rembrandt in London for five years, come back to America and worked at various jobs, then gone to London and auctioned the picture—shit, you can imagine all the this and that that'll have to be there. Imagine the flashback to Sotheby's with all the dealers sitting there making little gestures with their eyes and fingers, and the bidding goes up and up until the hammer comes down at one point three million dollars. And so the drama develops. Paul goes from success to success, you can imagine all the sex scenes, George plunges from failure to failure. Finally, George devises his revenge. Making friends with dropouts and sundry freaks who populate California, he forms a group of seven dedicated to the destruction of Paul, his mansion full of art, his family—convincing his disciples that Paul is a symbol of corruption in American civilization and he has to be sacrificed to purify the society, some such bullshit, you know how it is, I don't have to spell it out. They start digging a tunnel that finally leads beneath Paul's mansion. Above a party is in full swing, champagne is flowing, beautiful women are admiring Paul, below the guerrillas are tunnelling away. Well, the idea is not to do with the flamboyance and publicity with which urban guerrillas are more in love than with any meaning in their actions but to do it stealthily, subtly so that no one would know a crime had been committed. For George's idea is to give the impression that a sudden tremor has brought the mansion down, for he times the completion of his underground project to coincide with the beginning of the city's project to lay down new water-pipes five miles away where, George knows, they will be using dynamite, and he has calculated that the explosion of a certain quantity of dynamite five miles away will have the effect of producing the semblance of a tremor along the center of Paul's property, and with the foundations dug out, the final effect will be of the house appearing to be swallowed up by an earthquake. Oh, come on, I said to Jackie Gross as he told me this absolutely shitty story while trying to eat escargots which he called eska goats when ordering. Sure, he said, it's a neat plot, I'm trying to raise seventy-five grand for the property. Why, that's incredible, I said, I mean for this kind of . . . Yeah, he said, in his toneless voice, it's an extraordinary story with terrific opportunities for casting. And later when he was sipping coffee after threadbare Bernice Bauer had tried to burn a hole in his cheek, he said, Maybe I'll give her a part in one of the party scenes, but she'll have to mouth-wash me first.

—No shit! I cried. Did he say THAT?

—What did he mean by it, Walt? I asked him and he looked incredulously at me but merely shrugged his shoulders and lowered his eye-lids to his coffee and all I saw was that Brillo pad he wears for hair.

—Oh, it's nothing, I said, just an expression they have out here.

—What the hell does it mean, though?

—Shit, you know what mouth-wash means!

—You mean what you do with Listerine?

—Yeah, I said, you take it into your mouth and spit it out.

—Why, the dirty son of a bitch!

—This is California, sweetie, it's the end of the world. Their fantasies, reality and scripts are all mixed up and become more and more infantile as the sun seems increasingly distant beyond the thickening smog.

—Why, if I'd known, said Rosemary, I'd have stood up at once and walked right out. As it was when we left, there was Bernice Bauer with a young dark-haired starling named Everett Simpson at the door, just leaving too, and Bernice came up to Jackie Gross, saying, Ah must give a goodbha peck on mah fayvrut directah's cheek, and proceeded to put her arms around Jackie Gross and to give him a long kiss on the mouth, her shoulders working all the time so that the rockettes were firing away at Jackie's chest, while in the meantime young Everett Pimpson just stood there grinning at me. The valet brought Jackie's car, a '61 VW Bug that hadn't been washed for a decade, and saying goodbye to me, Jackie shot off into the smog. Imagine at that moment the astonishment on the faces of Bernice and her Pimple, for they had obviously expected Jackie to take me to his house and to put his head into my spittoon while I gave him a mouth-wash, but they quickly recovered their composure when their car, a '75 Riviera, was brought up, for Bernice said, Honey, we happen to be going your way, and invited me in. It was only when Everett had driven down three blocks that he turned round to me and asked where I wanted to go, and when I said L.A., he said, Of course that's where we're headed for. But he drove to Beverly Hills first, for Bernice suddenly declared she had a headache and had to go home. From there, Everett drove out to Santa Monica and began to head for Malibu, so that I said, What's the idea, I thought we were going to L.A., I've to be at the federal building by three.

156

And, Walt, do you know what that son of a Latin-haired bitch proposed?

—Oh, sure, you don't have to tell me, I said. I told you, this is the end of the world.

—But what's a girl supposed to do in this country, Walt? There's no honest old-fashioned lovers left who'll wear a white dinner jacket, listen to sad music on the piano and cry on your bosom, now all you get is guys with hairy chests, a gold chain hanging from the neck, and the first proposal they make to a girl is of some goddamn perversity. It's enough to break my virginal heart.

—Oh, come on, Rosemary, you've been around.

—Sure, I've been around, all the way from New York to L.A., via Texas and Montana, and there hasn't been a single guy who'll come to your bed with the decent idea of sleeping with you, instead there's these perversities.

—What was Everett's idea?

—I thought you didn't want to know, what are you, some kind of a voyeur, or something?

—No, I said, just thought it might be useful information. You're not obliged to tell me anything.

—He said if I wanted the hottest thrill in my life, I should insert jalapenos into my passage and he'd draw them out with his tongue, one by one, and eat them. It's strictly vegetarian, he added, but if you want meat I'll give you a rare piece later.

—And you told him to go to hell?

—Sure, that's exactly what I was going to tell him, but he was already driving on to the beach, saying I have a can of jalapenos at the back, and I thought, Well, no girl's going to lose her virginity having peppers sucked out of her in the back seat of a brand new Riviera.

—Rosemary!

—Why, Walt, have you offered me anything better? He had a half-gallon can of jalapenos back there.

—I've a file here on Everett Simpson.

—You may have the file, baby, but I have a fantastic memory. Thank God for General Motors, I say, they make back seats like

157

king size beds. Posturepedic, too. You can lie back in supreme comfort, throw your legs over the guy's shoulders and dig your heels into his back while he bends down there to work on the stuffed peppers, I've never been in such heat in my life.

—Please, Rosemary, spare me the details, leave it to my imagination, will you?

—Didn't think you had any, Walt, you spend too much time listening to your male friends' filthy stories.

—Here's the Everett file. Came into the country as a migrant worker, real name Carlos Zapateria.

—I don't believe that! Zapateria means a shoe shop, for god's sake!

—Maybe the officer who worked on the file didn't get on too well with foreign words. Anyway, Carlos picked cabbages on a farm near San Luis Obispo and was on a truck laden with cabbages one day when he saw a silver Lincoln stopped on the Pacific Highway with a flat, so he went and changed the tire for he'd seen a helpless middle-aged woman standing in front of the car with her hands on her hips. While he changed the tire, she took out her camera and shot a dozen pictures of him. She being a movie director's wife, the pictures were naturally seen by her husband who, as luck and happy coincidence once again would have it, was just beginning a movie with a Latin hero and was looking for a new face. There's a script of the movie here, too, it's about some Puerto Rican playboy who seduces a Boston Brahminette called Sally while she's vacationing in San Juan and after many humiliations ends up by marrying her and becoming a successful stock-broker in New York. Apparently, he hasn't made a movie since.

—It's tough living in an unpredictable economy, Rosemary said.

—Tough? Look, the guy only drives a brand new bordello on wide-track tires and independent rear suspension, I wouldn't feel sorry for him.

—I resent that remark, she said. Besides, it shows no respect for General Motors especially at a time when Detroit is in mourning.

—Okay, a goddamn hearse then!

—Now, Walt, it's no use losing your temper in these troubled times that have put the nation into an unprecedented crisis. Your obscenities will solve nothing.

—I suppose your example is what the nation should adopt. Okay, ladies, pull up your skirts and squirt salsa picante on your rose bushes.

—Walt, I've always lamented the sad fact that you have a filthy mind which obsessively and in an adolescent manner insists upon crazy distortions of the simple facts of life into obscene fantasies. If you only saw things the way they are, you'd have a healthier life.

—Thanks, lady. Hey, did you take that phone off the hook?

—Sure, as soon as I came in. You can't have a serious conference with the phone ringing all the time.

—Put it back, for god's sake, Rosemary!

—That's it, is it? You'd rather listen to some crank calling in to say there's a forest fire out on the ocean than hear my problems. You prefer to hear the D.A. shouting abuse on the phone or some narc giving the identities of fifty kids who smoked half a joint between them, shit, what kind of work is that? Whereas I'm talking about serious things. Jackie Gross said when he was trying to eat his goddamn eska goats, This business can only move forward if we get away from reality. Why, Jackie, I said, I didn't know you were a philosopher. It's nothing to do with philosophy, he said, tipping the snail to his mouth and dripping the butter all down his chin, it's a plain fact of the movie industry. A guy showed me a script the other day about a college kid who drops out in his sophomore year, becomes a rock superstar, wakes up one day to find himself thirty years old, hates his life of jets, women and heroin, gives it all up to go back to college where he switches majors from History to Business, graduates, gets a promising job with a starting salary of seven thousand a year, marries a simple farm girl from South Carolina and finds happiness in a mobile home. It's a swell idea, Rudi said to me when I'd read the script, hey, pal, he said, it'll bring them in all the way from Alaska to Texas, what do you say, Jackie? You know me, Rudi, I said, I gave up the corn business a long time ago, there's no money in it. Oh, come on, Jackie, Rudi said, this one will touch the nation's heart, it'll restore confidence in the great institutions of the country, it'll purify the waters of the Mississippi with the nation's tears. Relax, Rudi, will you? I said, hanging up, it just wasn't the kind of script I can work with, I'm a futurist.

—Ho, ho, Jackie Gross a futurist! I laughed. Did you see his last movie?

—Yeah, I saw it, Rosemary said. It was a futurist Western, men from Mars come down in their spacecraft and run into a horde of Apaches. It grossed twenty-five million, Jackie told me.

—Rosemary, do you mind putting that phone back?

—Not at all, she said, putting the receiver on its cradle.

I looked at the phone expecting it to ring out with twenty calls simultaneously but it remained silent, and Rosemary said, It's gone five, no one's going to call you now.

—What I fail to understand, Rosemary, is why you're so determined to destroy my career.

—You call it a career, sitting speaking to any crank who calls?

—Allow me to inform you that I've spoken today with the Governor of the state of California, the A.G. and the D.A., the District F.B.I, chief, the movie critic of the L. A. Times, a seismologist at Pasadena, an associate professor of History at U.C.L.A., the leader of a commune who'd come down to lecture at Irvine, the Executive Vice-president of United Artists and . . .

—Well, that just proves you take random shots in the dark and have no idea of what you're doing. You might as well sit at the movies all day. It's no wonder there's so much unsolved crime in this country. What do you do, go after imaginary leads?

—We solve some of the mysteries, sister, some of them, I said, abandoning all thoughts of rationalising my existence and work to Rosemary.

She seemed to sense that I wasn't going to argue any more and ceased making provocative statements, and said softly, You promised to take me to the beach after work, remember?

—Sure, I said, putting some papers in a tray on my desk.

—I know, she said. You work terribly hard and one day you'll even solve the mystery of life and death.

—Maybe, I said, walking out of the office with her.

—I suppose it's a matter of having contacts in the underworld, she said, laughing.

Outside the sun had broken through the smog and was shining from the roofs of thousands of cars which jammed the street. We joined the traffic in my Camaro and slowly made for the freeway to Santa Monica.

There were two million four hundred and sixty-nine thousand two hundred and eighty-three people on the beach at Santa Monica and we drove on toward Malibu.

Rosemary said: Jackie Gross thinks everyone has a script in them. You can't be serious! I said to him and he said, Why should I want to drop my ass in the gutter, I've a reputation to maintain. I can't even speak aloud, he added, there's always someone spying on me to get a futurist idea; for example, don't look now, but there's a guy at the next table, a journalist who keeps producing lousy scripts which no one wants, who's eavesdropping on us right now.

—Which reminds me, I said, slowing down behind a truck round a bend. It came to pass in the Garden of Eden that Eve being full in her belly of fruit, fish and fowl, could not contain herself any more and sat down under an almond tree in full blossom and the angel Gabriel observed her and when he later appeared before God and God asked Gabriel, What hast thou been observing Gabriel? And Gabriel said: Eve's droppings.

—Evacuation's the word, Rosemary said.

—And afterwards, she no doubt accused Adam of being full of shit, I said, at last overtaking the truck. What chance can men have in this country after that?

—Sure, Rosemary said, words are treacherous. But Jackie Gross said, The image can't represent anything but the capacity of the lens you use. Oh, I wouldn't agree with that, I said, for ideas don't come from a pen or a typewriter, and he said, But words don't have the framed definition of images on a screen, so I had to agree with him that if you work with a wide-angle you're going to get a wide perspective, and he said, Yeah, the wide-angle was great when we were on location in the desert, it kind of brought to the center what was in the corners of one's eyes.

The beaches were crowded all along the coast to Brookings in Oregon, so we turned back over the Siskiyou Mountains and drove down the Sacramento Valley. A narrow unpaved road which at one point had seemed the main passage led through vineyards and began to wind up a mountainside. We kept thinking that it would soon connect to a highway, for it had the appearance of the narrow gravel tracks improvised by highway engineers while they're working on a difficult stretch of road, but there seemed to be no end to the track we were on. The rocks and the gravel clattered against the underside of the car until the road became only two grooves in the dust. I didn't even have to steer. We must have climbed some, for around us now were pines, and as I was remarking upon this fact to Rosemary, although it was hardly worth doing so since she had obviously also witnessed the phenomenon, but we had to talk about something, the road suddenly ended. There were pine trees in front of us too. We got out of the car to stretch our legs. I observed there was no way I could turn the car around and would need to reverse a long way to find a sufficiently wide clearing. Just then an old man came out of the forest leading two mules and said, You'll need these now.

—What are you talking about? I asked.

—You've come so far, you're not going to give up now, are you? he asked.

—Of course not, Rosemary said.

—Well, the old man said, if you're not blind, you can see that this is where the road ends and you need mules if you're going to get anywhere.

—Why, of course, Rosemary said, we hadn't thought of that.

—Who are you? I asked the old man.

—The name's Matthews, he said, if it's any satisfaction to you. He led the mules up to Rosemary and me and we began to stroke their heads and to say such things to them as You're a sweet little boy, aren't you? Or, How are you, kid, like a lump of sugar? While we did so, we did not notice that the old man had got into the car, put it into reverse and begun to drive away.

—Hey! I shouted at him, running after the car for some twenty feet, Come back! But he vanished in a moment and even the cloud of dust settled to leave no trace of a car having been driven upon that track. When I walked back to the mules, Rosemary had already mounted hers and was saying, Come on, Walt, it's a fine view but we can't stand here all day.

Holding the reins, I put my left foot into a stirrup and as I did so, the mule began to walk briskly, so that I found myself stamping my right foot upon the ground, like a bicyclist does before flinging his leg over the saddle and sitting on it, in the process being both dragged by the mule and pushing him, and finally managed to heave myself up and to sit astride him. By the time I regained my breath, we were deep in the forest.

—Why're we going this way? I asked Rosemary who was ahead of me. We should have gone after the car.

—Don't be stupid, she said, he'd be in Tijuana by the time we got down to the river.

I didn't contest her logic, and in any case the mules appeared set in their ways and I suspected that nothing could have made them go in any other direction. The forest was thick with pines, dark and absolutely silent. No path had been worn upon the ground by former travellers, and yet I was not at all surprised to see arrow signs cut into the pines on my right at eye-level and nor was I surprised to discover that without any guidance from us the mules were clearly following the arrows. I asked myself why I wasn't surprised by these things but merely shrugged my shoulders when I had no answer, saying to myself that life was crazy, there was no explanation to any damn thing. Rosemary began to sing:

> High up in the pine forest
> Just below the snow-capped peaks
> The days are longer than nights
> And the nights are longer than weeks.
>
> High up in the pine forest
> Beneath the dark blue sky
> Where all there is is what
> And what there is is why.

—Jesus, Rosemary! I cried. You trying to drive me crazy or what? But she went on

> The castle has fallen, the prince
> And the princess are dead
> And from high up in the pine forest
> Even the evil witch has fled.

—Quit it, will you!
—What's bugging you, Walt?
—Do you mind telling me why you're so damned cheerful? We've lost our way, our car, our picnic basket with the cold roast beef in it, the cooler with the six-pack of beer, we have no expectation but to die, and you are singing away without a care in the world.

She turned her head back to look at me and said, What do you want me to do, reject the situation and make it worse?

—Just be realistic about it, I said.

—That's swell, she called back. I'll do just that when I need to amuse myself.

She halted, and did not respond to my retort that there was no call for irony. When I came to where she was, I too saw what had stopped her. There was a clearing ahead of us where an old man sat in front of a fire over which he held an iron skillet. An old woman stood beside him, her hands on her hips, and stared down at the fire.

—Hold it up a little higher, you ignorant prairie dog, the old woman said in a shrill voice, or you'll burn the bacon.

—I know what I'm doin', the old man said, lowering the skillet a couple of inches. You're a meddlin' old crow, he added.

—Your knowledge ain't worth a pig's ass, she said.

He flipped the bacon over and said, I'd fuck a pig's ass before your dry old . . . .

Just then they noticed us and not answering our greeting, the old woman said, Ya'll will be wanting to go that way, right opposite the setting sun. And she pointed a finger at the direction.

The mules apparently agreed with her, for they kept on going that way and would not be persuaded to pause again. The old man ran up to Rosemary with the skillet in one hand and held it up to her, saying, There's fried bacon and some bread, ya'll be wantin' to eat soon.

Rosemary touched the skillet's edge with a finger-tip and realizing that it was not going to scald her hand, she picked up the bread and the bacon from it, passing some to me. We thanked the couple for the timely assistance and carried on our journey.

We now seemed to be descending and the sun was directly behind us. There was maybe an hour to ninety minutes of daylight left. In a few minutes, however, we had descended sufficiently for the sun to be obscured by the eminence behind us, so that the light lost its brilliance and air became cool. Rosemary sang:

High up in the pine forest
I climbed nearly to the top
And although I needed rest
I just could not stop.

—Oh, Rosemary, cut it out, will you? Who taught you that song anyway?

—I don't know, Walt, it just comes to my mind by itself. You know, you ought to be more tolerant, you don't have to get so damned nervous, you're in America after all, the country is not going to eat you up.

We came to a cabin at nightfall on the edge of a stream, and it seemed fortunate that we should arrive there just when any further progress would have been impossible. The mules walked right up to the door of the cabin and stood there turning their heads to each other in a kind of congratulatory glance. God knows what was going on in their heads. Rosemary jumped off her mule, opened the door of the cabin and walked in as if it were her own cottage in the country.

—What are you doing, Rosemary? I called after her, dismounting with some difficulty. At least have the decency to ask if anyone is at home if you can't be bothered to knock.

—There would have been horses outside if anyone had been

here, she said when I joined her inside. A lamp hung from the ceiling and when I lit it we saw that there were two narrow beds with clean sheets and woolen blankets on them. There was nothing else in the cabin.

—It's perfect, Rosemary said.

—What do you mean? I asked. We can't sleep in those beds!

—You go and sleep out in the cold, if you like, she said, beginning to take off her clothes. And don't stand there staring as if you never saw a girl strip.

—I was just thinking you're okay.

—Sure, I'm okay, she said, just don't get any ideas, that's all.

—You have a fine couple of ideas right there, Rosemary, a good couple of notionettes.

—I told you, don't get fresh, she said, getting into bed. And you can turn off that light.

I, too, got into bed after turning off the light. It was comfortable and warm and I soon felt relaxed.

—It's like being home, I said.

But Rosemary had already gone to sleep.

I awoke early the next morning and saw the sun rising above the wide valley below, to my left, pink pools of light illuminating the vegetation and the meadows. To the right, the Rockies rose in picture-book formations, the blocked out deciduous areas beneath the white peaks; and above them the sky, gathering its blue in the morning light, sharpening in intensity with accustomed nonchalance. I thought of the prairie a thousand miles beyond the horizon and the great rivers that had their passage through it; and beyond that the other mountains and the timber forests and then the coastal plain, the east which had first declared the independent existence of America; and I thought of the plains of the south, the high plains of Texas, and then the rippling of the land, the tortured topography of the south that exhausted itself in the abstractions of the desert before acceding to tropical lushness. My mind beheld the land's intricacies, in that moment of the sun's rising and the sky's rinsing itself with blue and then a darker blue, with the Rockies behind me rising up out of the darkness.

I went to the stream and, lying on its bank, lowered my face to its rushing water, scooping up the water in cupped hands and splashing it to my face.

—So that's where you are! I heard Rosemary's voice behind me. I was afraid you'd taken fright and run away, she added, coming up to the stream, too.

—From this? I said, speaking into the clear, cool water in my hands.

—What have you found, gold? Rosemary asked.

—Maybe, I said, turning away from the stream and lying on the grassy bank, head propped upon a hand, the elbow in the grass, and scanned the horizon, looking for the deepest perspective. You know something, I said, I never did tell you the story of the Indian chief who gave me my liberty if I went in search of a beautiful princess who'd been lost as a baby. Poker always loved that story.

Afterword

by VANESSA GUIGNERY
Professor of English literature, École Normale Supérieure, Lyon,
France

I: A Short History of the Origin of
Hulme's Investigations Into the Bogart Script

On 24 November 1972, Zulfikar Ghose wrote to his friend the
American writer Thomas Berger:

> I started a new novel to be called HULME'S
> INVESTIGATIONS AND MY LADY INTRICATE.
> The last three words are from an e.e. cummings poem and
> my intention is to use several of his poems and also the
> poems of Crane, Stevens and Williams as a framework
> for this apparently mad work. As you know well, there's
> neither freedom nor rest for the writer, but a maddening
> compulsion which urges one to attempt further kinds
> of foolishness to prove one's absolute uselessness to the
> world.1

At that time, Ghose had been living in the United States for three
years, having immigrated in 1969 on being invited to teach in the
English department at the University of Texas at Austin. Born
in 1935 in Sialkot (in what was then India and would become
Pakistan after the Partition of 1947), Zulfikar Ghose moved to
Bombay with his family in 1942 and to England ten years later.
Between 1964 and 1967, he had published two collections of

---

1   All the letters from Zulfikar Ghose to Thomas Berger
quoted in this introduction are archived at the Harry Ransom
Humanities Center at the University of Texas at Austin (Reg. no.
15319).

poems, a precocious autobiography entitled *Confessions of a Native-Alien* (1965) and two realist novels, *The Contradictions* (1966) and *The Murder of Aziz Khan* (1967). The latter was deliberately written as a solid, straightforward novel to demonstrate that he could write in the traditional mould and therefore need not do it again but could turn instead to his real interest, which was to explore new literary forms. He proceeded to write *Crump's Terms*, which has stylistic affinities with the work of the French *Nouveau Roman* writers (Alain Robbe-Grillet, Claude Simon, Nathalie Sarraute) and which Macmillan, and several other publishers it was submitted to, rejected. Ghose thereupon conceived his major traditional work, *The Incredible Brazilian* trilogy, which so impressed Macmillan with its commercial potential that they agreed to Ghose's demand that they accept *Crump's Terms* as well. He said in an interview:

> If Macmillan had accepted [*Crump's Terms*] in 1968 when it was first offered to them, I would have progressed from there instead of spending the next eight years on the Brazilian trilogy. Who knows what I might not have discovered? The trilogy was amusing to write but it did not involve me in artistic growth. I suppose I began writing *Hulme's Investigations* before finishing the trilogy in order to console myself that I was not merely the writer of commercial fiction."2

Ghose's correspondence with Thomas Berger reveals some of his frustration with the composition of *The Incredible Brazilian* trilogy which was taking him away from more challenging aesthetic work. In a letter to Berger of 10 April 1973, he wrote: "Mentioning Crump reminds me that I read some of its pages the other day and was so impressed with some of its prose that I wondered why I was wasting my time with the Brazilian novel. The answer of course is money and also without the Brazilian I wouldn't have a publisher." In a letter of 14 May 1973 to B.S.

2   Chelva Kanaganayakam, "Zulfikar Ghose: An Interview", *Twentieth Century Literature* Vol 32, No. 2 (Summer 1986): 175.

Johnson, a writer who was constantly looking for new forms and patterns to try and reinvent the novel as a genre, Ghose referred to *Hulme's Investigations* and wrote: "This is more the kind of novel I want to write as opposed to the purely commercial thing like the Brazilian, and I think you'll approve of it when you see it".3 In a 2003 interview4 as well as in the essay 'How I Wrote Certain of My Books', reproduced in *In The Ring of Pure Light* (2011), Ghose recalls how he felt after he mailed the second volume of the trilogy, *The Beautiful Empire* (1972), to his agent:

> I experienced a fine sense of liberation when I drove away from the post-office, saying to myself that I would take a break from writing novels and work instead on some poems and essays. Arriving home, I entered my study, still enjoying the sensation of freedom. Then a strange thing happened. I sat down at my desk, inserted a piece of paper in the Smith-Corona and typed out the sentence, 'Finally we arrived in the desert.' I had no idea where that sentence had come from or what I was supposed to do with it. Who was represented by 'we', I wondered, and where was this desert? I needed more sentences to probe that mystery and typed out a few pages of them during the next few days.5

As noted by Ghose in another interview, that very first sentence, "Finally we arrived in the desert", "came with its buried hints and suggestions. It began to release an imagery of the United States, to which I was then a very recent immigrant."6 After

3   Vanessa Guignery, ed. The B. S. *Johnson – Zulfikar Ghose Correspondence* (Newcastle upon Tyne: Cambridge Scholars Publishing, 2015), 405.
4   Frederick Luis Aldama, "Crafting against the Grain: An Interview with Zulfikar Ghose", *The College English Association Critic*, Vol. 66, No. 1 (Fall 2003): 63.
5   Zulfikar Ghose, *In The Ring of Pure Light* (Karachi: Oxford University Press, 2011), 146.
6   Reed Way Dasenbrock and Feroza Jussawalla, "A Conversation with Zulfikar Ghose", *Op. cit.*, 152.

writing about the India of his youth in his 1965 autobiography and *The Murder of Aziz Khan*, and creating an imaginary Brazil – the home country of his wife Helena de la Fontaine – for the first two volumes of the trilogy, Ghose may have felt it was time to turn his attention to the United States, its myths, languages, literary traditions and popular culture for what could be called his "American novel"7. He described his new novel to Thomas Berger in a letter of 18 May 1974 as "an attempt to put together the images of America in my mind" in a way that was "quite wild, absurd, and, I hope, funny". As Ghose explained in an interview: "Some of the imagery in that novel was taken from nineteenth-century travel writing and journals and letters by people who were going west".8 In the essay from *In the Ring of Pure Light*, he gave more information about the extent of his borrowings, "pasting much of it down like a collage"9:

> I brought into my sentences unattributed appropriations of phrases from the American poets, especially Hart Crane – *O Nights that brought me to her body bare!*, he sings in an ecstasy of belonging to America – so that my prose, absorbing the words of Whitman, Stevens, Crane, was the poetry of America. Next, I brought in Hollywood in a series of remembered images of Humphrey Bogart movies [...]. Some sentences parodied the feverous pace of the fake seriousness of popular narratives.10

The novel thus clearly bears the marks of the extensive reading Ghose did in 1973-74. On 3 June 1974, he wrote to Thomas Berger:

---

7 Alamgir Hashmi, "Tickling and Being Tickled à la Zulfikar Ghose", *Commonwealth Novel in English* Vol. 1, No. 2 (July 1982): 157.
8 Reed Way Dasenbrock and Feroza Jussawalla, "A Conversation with Zulfikar Ghose", *Op. cit.*, 152.
9 *Ibid.*
10 Zulfikar Ghose, *In The Ring of Pure Light, Op. cit.*, 148.

I've been reading several books on the old West before continuing to write the rest of HULME. The most interesting reading is usually contemporary journals, diaries and letters. While reading these, and last year while reading similar books about Brazil, I was struck by the very fine prose some very prosaic people wrote in the nineteenth century. It's always clear, often very graphic and full of splendid images and vividly created details. It occurred to me that vividness in prose began to fade away with the coming of the camera; people treat each other to slide-shows but can't express two sentences with any clarity. As a consequence, the common run of writers are lazy, too, and have no facility for language and have lost the ability to be verbally inventive.

It is this verbal inventiveness Ghose aimed to achieve in *Hulme's Investigations Into the Bogart Script* and the book is remarkable indeed for the vividness of its images and details, sometimes with comic or parodic effects. For instance, when the narrator goes down the escalator in the London metro, he notices the framed ad "of bikini-bosomed Miss Nubilette Boobs in the Mediterranean at Tunis barely concealing her Christian boobiloos in a world of tense Arab timidity" (7)11 – an example of Ghose's playful alliterative prose – or in the Southwest, he views "[b]eyond the cedar and mimosa hill the fields of gaillardia, scarlet and yellow, whose pointillist intensity overwhelmingly routs the splashes of mauve and purple horsemint, verbena and spiderwort" (13).

As the quotations above suggest, Ghose's purpose was not to propose a realist fictional form nor to conjure up a nostalgic vision of some idealized West but to experiment with the limitless possibilities of language, an activity which brings him the type of aesthetic bliss writers like Nabokov or Flaubert rejoiced in, "that moment of ecstasy experienced by the mind when an expression, an image or a rhythm brings to it a sudden surge of pleasure".12

11   The page numbers are taken from the Curbstone Press edition of 1981.
12   Zulfikar Ghose, I*n The Ring of Pure Light, Op. cit.*, 3.

173

This primary interest in language became obvious to him as he went on writing the novel: "I soon realized that what I was trying to produce was a text which was simply a structure of language, which was not based on preconceived ideas, which was not trying to put forward the writer's views, which did not have a story or plot, but which was still fiction."13 In *Hulme's Investigations Into the Bogart Script* one therefore sees the realisation of the literary artist's ideal expressed by Flaubert when he wrote in a letter to Louise Colet on 25 June 1853: "I would like to produce books which would entail only the writing of sentences". As noted by Erwing Campbell, in this novel, "language qua language becomes the objective correlative of the work."14

In the summer of 1974, Ghose sent the first two thirds of the novel to his agent "hoping that he'd be sufficiently excited to show it to more than one publisher simultaneously, but he hasn't been too excited".15 On 25 October 1974, he wrote to Thomas Berger:

> Someone called Henry Robbins at Simon & Schuster turned down my new novel, the American one which in your case you have not seen.16 He thought it was fascinating but exasperating and couldn't tell what I was doing. Although I'd be glad for someone to take it, it pleases me that publishers are baffled by it. It could, of course, mean that the work is worthless, but to me it means that there's some originality in it. Eliot said somewhere that if someone immediately saw the point of a new poem

13   Chelva Kanaganayakam, "Zulfikar Ghose: An Interview", *Op. cit.*, 175.

14   Erwing Campbell, Review of *Hamlet, Prufrock and Language and Hulme's Investigations Into the Bogart Script*. *The Review of Contemporary Fiction* Vol. 3, No. 3 (1983): 226.

15   Letter to Thomas Berger, 16 November 1974.

16   The phrase "which in your case you have not seen" is a playful variation on a line repeated in Henry Reed's poem "Naming the Parts": "Which in our case we have not got". The use of that line in the correspondence with Berger became a joke between the two friends.

of his he'd be worried about the quality of the poem, and I sympathise with that.

On 6 January 1975, he described the book to his friend in the following terms: "It has no plot, is timeless, but I believe it's quite funny […] and I hope also philosophically not without meaning", but he also added: "The publishing situation being what it is, I do not expect anything to happen with it but do believe that in two or ten or twenty years it'll come out and mean something to someone." The book was indeed rejected by all the New York publishers to whom it was submitted. In the late 1970s however, one of Ghose's former students at the University of Texas, R. D. Taylor, had begun a publishing house named Curbstone Press. Reading his professor's novel in typescript, Taylor offered to publish it, and thus *Hulme's Investigations Into the Bogart Script* was brought out by Curbstone Press in 1981.

II: A Reading of *Hulme's Investigations Into the Bogart Script*

What happened after Ghose wrote that first sentence: "Finally, we arrived in the desert"? He wrote some more and, as the author recalls, "[t]he series of sentences seemed to suggest some event being narrated but the emerging narrative was being subverted by some of the sentences that, though one could not deny the logic of their presence, had no business to be there." From one point of view, the sentences "produced the illusion of a story being narrated", but from another, it felt that "it was nonsense".17 Ghose remarks in an interview: "And that is when I had the idea, what if you have a novel in which there are succeeding sentences, each one appearing to be logically succeeding the previous one, but soon the sentences, though still maintaining the appearance of logic, become disconnected from the first one. What happens then? And what happens to reality?"18 Ghose realized that while he had been writing the trilogy of *The Incredible Brazilian*,

17   Zulfikar Ghose, *In The Ring of Pure Light*, *Op. cit.*, 146.
18   Frederick Luis Aldama, "Crafting against the Grain: An Interview with Zulfikar Ghose", *Op. cit.*, 63.

composed as a traditional novel, his mind, "as a sort of suppressed rebellion, had quietly been working out a narrative pattern which was the very opposite of that traditional form, and no sooner had the trilogy been disposed of than the mind aggressively asserted its preference and [Ghose] found [him]self submissively following its dictation."19

A reader coming to *Hulme's Investigations Into the Bogart Script* without knowledge of twentieth-century movements that produced a wide range of experimental fiction but innocently opening it with the naïve expectation of being entertained by a distracting story, will perhaps be a little puzzled at first by the narrative's subversion of linearity. Several times, a story seems to begin but just as the reader becomes absorbed in it, the story takes an unexpected course that bears no temporal or historical relationship with its earlier part and yet there appears to be some logic to the illogic that infuses a dreamlike continuity to the disruption.

The clue to this technique is suggested in the novel's preliminary page headed 'Author's Note', which contains three epigraphs, of which the first is a memory of a text he has been unable to locate. After recording the remembered quotation, which, he says, it had been his desire to use as an epigraph to his novel but is not going to because he cannot confirm its source, and thereby doing so while pretending he is not, he refers to "Stendhal's example in *Le Rouge et Le Noir* where several epigraphs are themselves fictions", thus implying that that is exactly what he himself has just done. And, maintaining the pretence that he is particular about quoting only that to which he can attribute a verifiable source, he then adds quotations from Malcolm Lowry and Ludwig Wittgenstein.

The 'Author's Note' appears to be a playful intellectual engagement with the reader, and while there may be clues in the first two quotations – the unverified one and Lowry's, which point to what the reader might expect in the novel –, it looks as though by keeping Wittgenstein's statement (from his philosophical work *On Certainty*) to the end, Ghose wants Wittgenstein's remark, *"what we believe is not a single proposition, it is a whole system of*

19   Zulfikar Ghose, *In The Ring of Pure Light,* Op. cit., 146.

propositions", to remain foremost in the reader's mind. His novel is indeed to be perceived as a series of propositions which singly do not picture a meaningful reality but do so when they are all experienced as a whole system. Furthermore, some readers will be reminded that one of Wittgenstein's posthumous works is titled *Philosophical Investigations* (1953), and that, therefore, it is conceivable that Ghose intended the *Investigations* in the title of his novel to have a philosophical resonance and thereby release an association in those readers' minds of the name *Hulme* being that of the philosopher, T. E. Hulme (1883-1917),[20] whose "Essays on Humanism and the Philosophy of Art" were published in a volume titled *Speculations* (1936). Ghose draws attention to the novel's philosophical foundations in his essay, 'How I Wrote Certain of My Books':

> Writing those sentences that led to the creation of a character named Hulme, the conspiracy that had been elaborating itself in my mind – that unconscious rebellion – became clear and I understood what this new novel demanded I do: if the apprehension of reality is a structuring of speculative propositions, then the assumption of truth is only a confirmation of belief induced by correct grammar, and if this is so, can one not have a succession of sentences which, though seeming to suggest a continuous set of events propelled by a Newtonian cause and effect dynamic, contained a subversion of time and space and mimicked Heisenberg's universe where there was no certainty, only propositions for Wittgensteinian analysis?[21]

In *Hulme's Investigations Into the Bogart Script*, the character Hulme who appears as a shadowy and elusive figure is presumed <u>to be a detective</u> whose interest in investigative procedures, it is

20   T. E. Hulme is remembered more as a poet than as a philosopher. Though he wrote very few poems, his founding contribution to the Imagist movement, which was adopted by Ezra Pound, is of seminal significance to modern English poetry.

21   Zulfikar Ghose, *In The Ring of Pure Light, Op. cit.*, 147.

hinted, is not to solve some crime but to decipher the enigma of existence. There is an obvious play on the pronunciation of his name, which when printed without the *l* still sounds the same but identifies him as the supreme empiricist David Hume, and reinforces the hint that the detective's magnifying lens is focussed upon examining clues that might settle the epistemological turmoil in the human mind.

Epistemological speculation has been a dominant preoccupation in Ghose's books of literary criticism, which, from the first, *Hamlet, Prufrock and Language* (where Wittgenstein and F. H. Bradley provide the philosophical basis for Ghose's interpretive analysis), and on to the sixth, *In the Ring of Pure Light*, are all concerned with the artist's manufacturing of reality as a fiction representing his essential vision. His poetic and fictional work also regularly raises philosophical questions: even in *The Incredible Brazilian*, which Ghose himself calls a 'traditional' mainstream novel, there are passages where the hero Gregório is engaged in a philosophical discussion, and in the final volume of the trilogy, entitled *A Different World* (1978), the 'Proem', 'Interlude' and 'Coda' chapters are conspicuously composed in a deliberately poetical prose where the ideas are philosophical. It is not surprising, therefore, that behind the surface narrative chaos of *Hulme's Investigations Into the Bogart Script*, a novel which is "an investigation into the self's relationship with the reality in which it found itself",22 should be a serenely composed philosophical design seeking to establish a meaningful order on the confusion experienced as reality.

In Ghose's twenty-five books written over half a century, another recurrent theme has been the loss of his homeland, whether in his poetry, beginning with his first book of poems, *The Loss of India* (where he has lost India, and India him, and India becomes the symbol of the dispossessed land), his second novel, *The Murder of Aziz Khan* (with its concluding image of Aziz Khan staring at his stolen land from behind a barbed-wire fence), or again in *Hulme's Investigations Into the Bogart Script*, a liberating quest in the discovery of a new land. As Ghose shaped

22   *Ibid.*, 148.

vivid images in a succession of sentences, he became aware that

> […] another activity of the unconscious mind began to manifest itself: that pattern which is a sort of watermark of the individual self began to reveal itself, images that comprise a matrix of the self's obsessions and are charged with archetypal force stampeded out of my brain. Ah, yes, that old pain of deracination, that exile from my native habitat, that original expulsion from paradise, and this arrival in the New World, my America, my new found land, to which I was a recent immigrant. […] behind the disruptions of continuity created by sentences that had the appearance of being normal there was a story of the tormented self, the soul in exile that looked apprehensively at the new landscape, willing it to be paradise and fearful that it might be not […].23

Right at the end of the novel, the narrator, Walt, awaking one morning among the Rockies, has a vision of all of America, and his companion Rosemary finding him lying on the bank of a stream scooping up water from it and splashing it on his face, asks, "What have you found, gold?" and he answers, "Maybe" and then turning away from the stream and "lying on the grassy bank, head propped upon a hand, the elbow in the grass, [he] scanned the horizon, looking for the deepest perspective" (158). In this conclusion and throughout the book, the reader can visualize scenes that had been described by the early chroniclers of America, hear the rhythm and tonalities of nineteenth-century American poems, recall shots from popular movies and westerns, while all the time being aware of the author's deliberate exposure of his parodic intent. To quote Erwing Campbell, Ghose

> […] sifts the detritus of popular culture and genre fiction, like some French *bricoleur*, for the materials with which to construct his novel: cowboys and Indians, gangsters and detectives, the clichés of uncounted movies, paperback

23   *Ibid.*, 147-48.

novels, television series, and radio dramas – predictable forms selected not for their commercial value, but for the universal expectations they generate, expectations which when subverted force the reader into an unaccustomed role in order to do justice to the implicit and the unknown.24

Hulme's Investigations Into the Bogart Script, a novel characterized by its wild humour (through wordplay, puns and parodic situations), often takes the reader by surprise, frustrating expectations and offering original perspectives instead. The fictionality of the text is exposed with such metatextual comments as Walt's memo to Hulme – "The story can develop complications, twists, surprises, while pursuing the mule's-track of clichés down the narrow ravine of public taste, though I admit this mode of expression is degenerate to say the least" (85) – or the note the narrator is given: "Not too promising. Situation too predictable, moral direction obvious. No doubt new characters will be introduced" (74). After imagining what new characters and twists to the plot could be added, the note concludes with a remark which brings the reader back to the novel's principal concern: "Though of course everything depends on style" (75).

---

24   Erwing Campbell, *Op. cit.*, 226.

About the Author

Photograph by Helena de la Fontaine

Zulfikar Ghose is internationally known as a critic, poet and novelist. His books include *Jets from Orange*, *Figures of Enchantment* and a trilogy, *The Incredible Brazilian*. His work has received praise from T. S. Eliot, Anthony Burgess, John Fowles and Michael Moorcock, amongst others.

Born in 1935 in Sialkot, Pakistan, Ghose emigrated to England in 1952. After graduating from Keele University with a BA in English and Philosophy, he lived in London where he was a cricket correspondent for *The Observer* and wrote for the *Times Literary Supplement*, *The Spectator* and the *Western Daily Press*.

In 1960, he met the novelist and poet B. S. Johnson, with whom he became close friends, and in the same year he joined The Group – a collection of poets who met at Edward Lucie-Smith's house in Chelsea to discuss their work. These meetings were attended by, amongst others, George MacBeth and Philip Hobsbaum, and occasionally by Ted Hughes.

In 1963, Zulfikar Ghose was put forward for the E. C. Gregory Award by the judges T. S. Eliot, Herbert Read, Henry Moore and Howard Sergeant; but when Eliot fell ill, his place on the committee was taken by a solicitor who raised an objection concerning Ghose's nationality. The committee decided to overcome the legal hurdle by giving him a "Special Award". His works comprise books and poems published on both sides of the Atlantic and where his rich prose has been described as "remarkable, imagistic, witty and original" and all his writing "sheer literary pleasure, exciting, effective, evocative and the beauty of great art".

In 1969, Ghose emigrated to the U.S.A after an invitation to teach at the University of Texas at Austin. He had tea with Patricia Nixon at the White House who presented him with a copy of *The Complete Poems of Elizabeth Bishop*. He became a US citizen in 2004 and went on to hold the distinguished position of Susan Taylor McDaniel Regents Professor in Creative Writing. Ghose, now retired from full-time teaching, is the Professor Emeritus, University Texas at Austin.

He lives with his wife Helena de la Fontaine, an artist from Brazil, whom he married in London in 1964.